LAKE EFFECT DAYS

LABORATORY
BOOKS
ASTORIA
QUEENS

LAKE EFFECT DAYS

WRITTEN AND ILLUSTRATED BY

PHILIP SULTZ

BRIEF STORIES

Stories from this collection have appeared in the following publications.
The Doctor T. J. Eckleburg Review (May 2014): "Sauce"
Everyday Genius (June 2011): "Stan," "Stones"
Fifth Wednesday Journal (Fall 2012): "Big Deal," "Billboard," "Boris," "Diner," "ESP," "The Farm," "Greens," "Joey's," "Lisa," "The List," "Millie," "Model," "Nate," "Need," "The Park," "Signs," "Tree Farm," "Venice," "Voice," "Wild"
The Hopkins Review (Spring 2016): "Afternoon Tea," "Bananas," "Benny," "The Boxer," "The Doctor," "Elastics," "Hitchhiker," "Joel," "Noël," "Noodles," "Pie Truck," "Salesmen," "Shoes," "Stew," "Three," "Vinnie"
Matchbook (Fall 2011): "Loops," "Lunch"
The Three Quarter Review (March 2012): "The Plan," "Spaghetti Run"

Laboratory Books LLC
35-19 31st Avenue, No. 4R
Astoria, NY 11106
www.laboratorybooks.xyz

First edition
10 9 8 7 6 5 4 3 2 1

ISBN 978-1-946053-09-1

Library of Congress Control Number: 2018947609

Text set in Balboa and Electra LT

Printed in the Czech Republic

CONTENTS

INTRODUCTION

It all began in Buffalo between World War II and the Korean Conflict, as it was called, when the guys would meet up late at night in a diner for their brand of fellowship. They were mostly high school graduates in their late teens and early twenties, the sons of immigrant families. It didn't matter; there was little trace of that showing. They didn't look or act alike, but they had a sense of who they were, sort of proud for some reason, without much to show for it. Some of them had jobs or worked in the family business, or were brewing up something to make a quick buck, and some were moving toward an inscrutable life as a scholar or an artist. After the Second World War, the world changed quickly. Early on, Arnie was top dog. He had a car, or his old man's, and they drove into the darkness late at night on the edges of Buffalo talking about girls, money, sports, jobs, or sat in silence riding into the future. Some of the guys smoked cigarettes, but there was no booze or dope. Maybe their background had something to do with it. They were more likely to pull into a late-night hot dog stand. Some of them were drafted into the army and went their own way after that.

BIG DEAL

I hear about him months before I meet him. A couple of guys are playing handball in the park. I'm watching. He comes up to me and says, You Sultz? I say, Yeah. He says, I'm Arnie. I hear you drive a truck. I say, My dad has a truck. I drive his pickup. Arnie says, Somebody said you drove a big truck. I say, I drove a bakery truck one summer, that's all. He says, Well look, I'm planning to build bomb shelters, and I need someone to drive a cement mixer. It's simple, they load you up at the cement factory, and you drive the truck to the site. I say, Arnie, I can't help you. Okay, Arnie says, I wanted to give you first crack at it. There's good money in this. I'm getting the Department of Defense blueprints any day now, and we're going to make a lot of them. There's a lot of fear out there. I say, Well yeah, I guess. Arnie says, I hear you're an artist. Do you sell anything? I say, I'm just getting started. Doesn't sound good, Arnie says. I think you're in the same pickle my friend Mel is in. He's going to be a philosopher.

Weeks later I run into Arnie. He says, Hey, you want to have lunch? I'll buy you a hamburger. We're driving along, and then he pulls into the big city cemetery. I say, What's up, somebody die? Arnie says, No, I just want to see something. He drives slow, then stops and gets out. He walks around, and then just stands there. Then he gets back in the car. I say, You looking for someone? He says, Cemeteries only get bigger. You can make a fortune growing grass. You know what I'm talking about, chunks that you lay in there. I say, Yeah, I think I've seen that. Sometimes they come in rolls. Arnie says, Yeah, that's it. Lets get some lunch.

STORE GUARD

Arnie works a deal. He's been managing a discount women's clothing store for a few months. He phones me and says, Look, we're having a Saturday sale today. My guy didn't show up. I need a store guard for the day. You'll make twenty bucks. Can you help me out? You just stand around. If you see anyone stealing, you let me know. I'll give you a whistle.

I come down. Arnie gives me a whistle and I stand around. After a while I see a woman walking out of the store with clothing still on the hanger. I blow the whistle. Arnie catches up with her. She tells him that she wants to show her husband the dress and he's sitting in the car. Arnie says, There's a lot of that, and anyway, I'm getting out of this deal.

We leave the shop toward evening. It's August, so it's still light out. Arnie drives to an old ritzy neighborhood north of the city. He drives slow, up one street and down the next, looking at the mansions, and the big trees and lawns. He says, I want one of these. I say, Lots of grass to cut. He says, If you got one of these, somebody else cuts the grass. He pulls into the driveway of one of the mansions, and goes to a side door with an envelope. When he returns, I say, Who lives here? He says, The owner of the clothing store. I just quit. I say, You just quit? Arnie says, You feel like pizza? I say, Sure. He says, Let's get some. It's on me.

JOEY'S

I get a second-shift job on a punch press. The factory is close by. I walk down after to Joey's Diner. Arnie and the guys are there shooting the breeze. Arnie says, Hey, what's up? I say, Nothing's up. Arnie says, Moe and Barney are talking about pooling their money to buy a scrapyard from one of the uncles. A lot of talk. I say, I'm getting coffee. Arnie says, You ever had a cube steak sandwich? I say, Is it shaped like a cube? Arnie says, No, it's a square. Arnie hollers, Hey, Joey, make us two cube steak sandwiches. I say, You don't have to do that, I'm working. Arnie says, Yeah, but you always just get coffee. You trying to save for something? I say, I got another year of art school. Art supplies make you poor. Arnie says, Why don't you just do that on the side? That's a road to nowhere. I know it's important to you, but you got to have clothes and a nice car if you want a broad. Hey, I got an idea, short-termwise. We get an easel and take it over to the beach. I'll drum up the crowd. We'll make some signs and charge five bucks. You can draw their heads or what do you call them, profiles. I say, I'm not good at that. Arnie says, What do you mean? Look, Sultz, never put yourself down, even if you have to lie. I say, I don't like sitting in the sun. Arnie says, I'll get you an umbrella. I say, Let's change the subject. I ask Arnie if he's still stuck with the bomb shelter cement. He says, Yeah, I got another week to pick it up, or I break the contract. Our sandwiches come. Arnie says, Hey, Sultz, don't you have an uncle who puts up houses? I say, Yeah, my uncle Sam. Arnie says, I'll make him an offer for the cement.

STONES

Arnie calls late one night. He says, You want to go for a hot dog? I say, Yeah, sure. We drive around town for quite some time. I say, So where's the hot dog? He says, I got to pick up something first. He pulls into a driveway. A guy comes out of a small house with a cardboard box. Arnie opens the trunk and they talk for a minute. Now there are three boxes in the trunk. He pays the guy, and we leave. Arnie says, The guy has a pit in the back. I buy stones from him every few months. I say, What kind of stones? He says, They're little white stones. They're considered semiprecious. We get to the hot dog stand. He opens the trunk and shows me the stones. I say, Arnie, as far as I know, semiprecious stones are polished, and these are just little white stones. He says, There's a market for it. There's a guy with a store full of smelly candles and beads and stuff who'll buy them. He sells them to arty people. He thinks they're special. I make good money with this. They glue them onto metal, like pendants. Arnie says, You got to keep your eyes open. You could have a potential oil gusher in your backyard and not know it. I say, How did you know about the stones? He says, I sold him the house. We were walking around and I saw a few white stones. So I told him, if there are more, throw them in a box, I'll shell out a few bucks. So he does.

BUFFALO

Moe says, Arnie, do you know what year your folks came over from the old country? Arnie says, I'm not sure, Moe, probably late teens, early twenties. I think they were right behind yours. Barney says, They must have all had the same travel brochure. Moe says, Like them reindeer up in Finland, following the ones in front of them. Arnie says, Some were already here sending money back for boat fares. The ones over there figured, If they can pay for my boat fare, they must be doing pretty good. Anyway, a lot of them went to other places, not just Buffalo. Moe says, Somebody must have wised them up. Barney says, Buffalo ain't so bad. We got lots of attractions. Moe says, Name one. Barney says, Maybe they heard of Freddies Doughnuts. I go out of my way for one of them glazed doughnuts. One of them and a cup of java is the perfect snack. The guys laugh. Moe says, Thousands of cars come to Buffalo every summer on their way to Niagara Falls, whether they want to or not. Barney says, Maybe there ain't a lot of great attractions right in the city, but there's good places around it, like Ebenezer, for one. Arnie says, What's in Ebenezer besides a Boy Scout camp and a lot of trees? Barney says, I liked that Boy Scout camp a lot. Arnie says, Yeah, when you were twelve. Moe says, If those immigrants knew about Florida, they might have gone there. Arnie says, Florida was after the war. Nobody went there before the war. Moe says, How come? Arnie says, Air conditioning came in after the war. Barney says, The grass is always greener somewhere else. Moe says, Yeah, grass. I remember grass. It comes up in April when the snow melts. The guys laugh.

THE LIST

I don't have bus fare. I walk through the park. It cuts out a half mile. When I get to the art school, a police officer at the entrance asks me for identification. I hand him my Social Security card. He says, You're under arrest on suspicion of burglary. I say, What burglary? The police officer says, Save it for the station. He handcuffs me and says, Get in the back seat of the patrol car. We get to the station, walk to the desk, and the sergeant behind the desk says, You're allowed one phone call. I call Arnie and tell him I'm at the Delaware Police Station, arrested on suspicion of burglary. He says, I'll be right down. They take the handcuffs off and take me to a room with a table and two chairs, and a camera attached to the wall. After a few minutes, a detective and a police officer come in. The police officer stands by the door. The detective and I sit at the table opposite each other. The detective says, I have a list of three burglary suspects and you're one of them. The art school office was robbed yesterday and four hundred dollars and a typewriter were stolen. I say, Why am I on the list? The detective says, There is evidence based on your behavior provided to us by a school source. I say, What school source? Am I dreaming or what? The detective says, Yeah, I hear you. It's tough all over. He says, Where were you between five yesterday afternoon and seven this morning? The door opens, and Arnie and Marvin, his lawyer, enter the room. Marvin says, My client will attend the court hearing at the assigned date, at which time we will present our case. The detective says, Okay, pay the bond at the desk and you're free to go. Arnie pays a thousand dollar bond and we leave the station. I talk to Marvin. He says, Okay, I have your word, just go on with your life. The school's blowing off steam. We'll keep in touch. Arnie says, Marvin, thanks for the quick response. Marvin says, We'll wrap this up, pronto. I'll talk to you soon.

Arnie drives to Joey's and we have breakfast. Arnie says, With all the people there, why are they picking on you? I say, It's not just me, it's two others. Arnie smiles and says, Hey, what have you been up to? I say, Thanks for coming down and paying the bond. Maybe I'm on their list because I sweep the floors after school. The office door isn't locked. The students are gone. It's just some staff and maintenance people in the building. Arnie says, Put it out of your mind. Enjoy your breakfast. The head guy or his secretary left money around, so now they're shooting in the dark. They pick three guys out of a hat. At least they think you're smart enough to pull off a job. That takes planning. I say, Arnie, I plan other things, not robberies. Arnie says, Forget it, they can't prove anything. Look at the bright side. When word gets out that you're a burglary suspect, you're going to attract a few chicks out of this. I say, Yeah, sure. The next day after school, I go to the broom closet to sweep the floors and run into the building superintendent. He's angry. He says, Hey, where were you yesterday? You missed a school day and you didn't notify me ahead of time you weren't going to show up. There's no excuse for that. I say, I was down at the . . . He says, Never mind where you were at. You miss another day, and you're through working here.

NOODLES

Barney calls Moe and says, You eat yet? Moe says, No, what's up? Barney says, There's a new Italian restaurant around the corner from me. They got special steak plates. Moe says, So what's new about steak? Barney says, It comes with noodles and a meat sauce. You ever hear of that? Moe says, No, I don't go for that. You buy a steak, you're supposed to get a baked potato. When you switch off from chewing meat, you follow it up with a baked potato. Barney says, These noodles are called pasta. They're long and chewy. Moe says, I seen that in a restaurant. I don't like bending over and slurping my food in. Barney says, Moe, they don't do that. They wind it around a fork, sitting in a big spoon, then they eat it from there. Moe says, Sounds nutty. Barney says, I guess that way they don't do a lot of slurping. You want to give it a shot? No one's going to watch you, they got booths. Moe says, No, I'm not in a steak mood. I'm thinking like a bowl of hot chili tonight. Fire up the gums with soda crackers and an ice cold pop. You know what I mean? Like a challenge. Barney says, I hear you. Stick with the basics. Sounds good. I'll join you.

ESP

Arnie phones. His neighbor's German shepherd ran off some-where. Arnie's into extrasensory perception. He explained it to me once. I listened patiently and acted as if I was inter-ested, but I thought it was a lot of baloney. In a serious voice, Arnie says, Can you see anything? I say, Yeah, I see a church and a wrought iron fence. He says, I'll pick you up in ten minutes. I say, I was just kidding, but he's already hung up. Arnie grew up in this part of town, so he has some place in mind. He picks me up and we drive a couple miles and then walk to the corner and look across the street at a church with a wrought iron fence. The German shepherd is standing next to the fence. Arnie acts like this is all natural. We take the dog back. Before he drops me off, he says, Promise me you won't send me any ESP messages unless we both agree beforehand. I say, Yeah, sure. I get a phone call a few days later. Arnie's upset. He says, I thought we agreed not to send messages to each other. I say, I didn't. Arnie says, Look, just knock it off.

A few weeks later, Arnie calls and wants me to go to the horse races with him. I say, What do you want me to do, pick the winners? Arnie says, You can do it if anyone can. All you have to do is relax and not force it. Let it just come to you, like you did with the German shepherd. I say, Arnie, that was just a lucky coincidence. Arnie says, I'll pick you up at ten on Saturday.

We're in the stands. I'm thinking this is nutty. I look at the list of horses in the first race and tell Arnie what I see for win, place, and show. Arnie puts bets on all three spots. Now the horses are racing down the track, and they come in just like I told him, and we're both laughing. Arnie places bets on the next race and I'm thinking we're going to make a lot of money, but only the second-place horse comes in. From then on everything falls apart. Arnie stops betting after a couple more races and says, The trouble with you is that you're thinking. You're not supposed to think. I say, Arnie, I didn't know I was thinking. Arnie says, Forget it, let's take off.

POP'S PIES

Speakers are invited to the fourth grade class to talk about the work they do. Ann's Uncle Barney comes on a Monday, one of his days off. He's wearing Pop's Pies overalls with a pie picture on his back and *Pop's Pies* printed on the front. The speakers introduce themselves and then the children raise their hands and ask questions. Barney has brought samples of the three pies they make. He cuts the saucer-sized pies in half pieces to hand out later. The teacher says to Barney and the class, Thank you, Mr. Field, for taking the time to come to our school. Then Barney gets up from his chair in front of the class and says, Well, I think most of you know I work at Pop's Pies, because of what I'm wearing, so you can just raise your hand if you have a question. A kid asks, Where do the pies come from? Barney says, They come from the pie factory where they're baked. Another kid asks, Who makes the pies? Barney says, There's four ladies who work the second shift who make the pies. Another kid asks, What's a second shift? Barney says, The ladies work from four to midnight. It's called the second shift. Another kid asks, What are the pies made of? Barney says, The pies are made of dough with fruit in them. Another kid asks, What's dough? Barney says, Dough is what holds the pie together. Another kid asks, Isn't dough made from flour? Barney says, Yeah, dough is made from flour. That's right. Another kid asks, Where's the flour come from? Barney says, The flour comes from farms that grow the wheat. Another kid asks, Where do you come from? and the kids laugh. The teacher says, Charles, behave yourself, or I'm going to ask you to leave the room. Barney smiles and says, I come from the pie truck. Another kid asks, What kind of pies do you deliver? Barney says, We make three pies, apple, cherry, and pineapple. In the fall, we also make pumpkin pie for Thanksgiving. Another kid asks, Which is your favorite? Barney says, I like them all. Another kid asks, How do you keep the pies from falling apart when they're in the truck? Barney says, That's a good question. The dough covers the whole pie, so after they cool, there's a machine that takes them on a conveyor belt and slides them into a cellophane bag and folds it. Then the pies are put on trays that go on racks in the truck. Another kid asks, What's a conveyor belt? Barney says, It's the moving part of the machine that takes the pies on wide belts across the room. Another kid asks, Who runs the machine? Barney says, Al runs the machine. He's been there since they started making pies. Another kid asks, How many trucks do you have? Barney says, We have three trucks. Another kid asks, Where do you take the pies? Barney says, We take them all over the city to different grocery stores, and some restaurants. Another kid asks, Who is Pop? Barney says, Pop is Irwin Ross. He's the owner. Another kid asks, Why do you call him Pop? Barney says, I'm not sure. I guess because it goes with pies. Another kid asks, Did you go to school to do this? Barney says, No, there ain't no school for this except you got to have a license to drive a truck. The kids are quiet and Barney turns to the teacher and says, If we could make a line, I'll give everyone a sample of the pie they want. The teacher says, Let's thank Mr. Field for being with us, and telling us about his interesting occupation, and the kids holler, Thank you, Mr. Field, and they get in line.

SPAGHETTI RUN

Arnie calls. He says, You ever been to New York? I tell him,
Not yet. He says, I'm going tomorrow, do you want to go? I
say, Sure. He picks me up and we drive all night. We hit a few
rest stops, and then as it gets light, we approach the city. He
says, Skyscrapers, Sultz. There's a lot to see. Arnie keeps driving around. I thought he had something to do here. He says,
What do you want to do, Sultz? I say, I don't know, maybe
walk around, look at the Empire State Building, maybe take
a picture. I tell him I borrowed a Brownie camera, but I need
film. He gives me money for film and finds a parking space.
I buy film and take a picture of the Empire State Building.
We walk close by and have a thirty-five cent plate of spaghetti
and meatballs, and then he says, I got enough money for gas,
and so we head back to Buffalo. He says, What do you think
of New York, Sultz? I say, Yeah, they have good spaghetti. He
says, You ever been to Niagara Falls?

THE FARM

Most everything with Arnie involves driving. It's not that he's happy when he's driving, it's just what he mostly does. He's poker-faced about it, as he is about things in general. Now he's doing real estate this week for someone, or himself. I don't ask. I'm sure he likes the driving part. He calls me up. He says, Sultz, do me a favor. Are you free for a couple of hours? I say, What's going on? He says, I'm looking at a piece of property out of town, a farm and some acreage. While I'm talking to the owner I want you to walk around, like you know about farms. I got a straw hat that you can wear, like you're a country guy. Look up and down at the doors and windows and so on, while I'm talking to the guy. Then come back in a few minutes and pull me aside like you're giving me the low-down. He'll think you're talking about the weaknesses. Then I'll do the rest. I say, Arnie, I'm not good at that sort of thing. He says, You'll do fine, buddy. I'll be right over. We drive out to the farm. A man in overalls appears and shakes hands with Arnie. I walk around wearing the straw hat like I'm looking at something. I walk up to the main barn, and a boy, maybe twelve, comes out of the barn door and says, You looking for something, mister? I say, No, I'm just looking at the barn. The boy says, What are you looking at the barn for? The man talking to Arnie hollers, Hey Jimmy, he's with this man here. A big shaggy dog comes out of the door and jumps up on me and leaves dirt on my shirt. The boy says, He's friendly, mister, he won't hurt you. When your shirt dries, you can just brush that cow dung off. You want to buy eggs, mister? I say, How much are they? He says, They're fourteen dollars a gross. I say, How many in a gross? He says, Mister, you don't know that? Arnie yells, Let's go, Sultz. I head back to the car.

Driving out, Arnie says, It's a working farm. He knows what he's got. I say, I think the kid had my number. Arnie says, Yeah, Sultz, you were just supposed to walk around and come back. What's that smell?

ANNA

Coming home, Arnie's car breaks down near Rochester. He calls me. I borrow my dad's car and drive the sixty miles, see Arnie, and pull behind his car. I say, What happened? Arnie says, I think it's something to do with the ignition. I say, Who's in the back seat? Arnie says, Her name is Anna, she's a relative on my mother's side. She's been staying with a distant relative here, but she works all day, and it wasn't working out. Jane wants her with her. Arnie calls Rochester AAA and has his car towed to his dealership in Buffalo. Arnie and Anna get in the car, and we head back. I turn toward the back seat and say hello. She doesn't say anything. She looks like she could be in her early forties, skinny, thick glasses, but a nice face. Arnie says, She knows a few English words. She's Polish. She survived the war somehow. Nazis broke into her house and shot her husband and two kids when she was delivering eggs to the house of a Christian neighbor. They hid her under a trap door in the kitchen floor for months. It's a long story. I say, Wow, what a nightmare. Arnie says, There's a program for victims of the war in Buffalo, and hopefully she can find a way to live again. I say, Does she have any skills? Arnie says, Her papers say *farmer's wife*. They had chickens and geese. She made goose-down pillows. I say, They worked with what they had. Arnie says, I don't think she'll be doing that in Buffalo. When we arrive, I say, Anna, welcome to Buffalo. I think she gets the idea, maybe not. Jane comes out, and they hug and kiss each other, and Jane begins to cry. Anna takes a handkerchief and wipes the tears from Jane's face.

HOME

We come out of the restaurant. As usual, Arnie pays. I say, Thanks, Arnie. Arnie says, The place has gone down. I say, You come here often? Arnie says, Now and then. They've been pretty good up until now. Who knows, maybe a different chef. I say, Or a lower grade of beef. Arnie says, Yeah, it could be. You can go to the same restaurant and order the same thing, be happy one day and disappointed the next. Explain that. I say, It could be you. You have a taste for something one day, and the next time you don't. Do you ever eat at home? Arnie says, Yeah, sandwiches, takeout stuff. I never use the stove except to boil water or heat soup. I say, You could do better than that. Arnie says, Do you cook stuff? I say, No, but I can make a cheeseburger. Arnie says, How do you do that? I say, You put cooking oil in a frying pan on a moderate flame for a minute, put a meat patty in the pan, check to see if the other side is brown, then flip it over. You let the other side get brown, and then you put a slice of cheese on top of the burger, wait a minute for it to melt a little, open your bun, and you got a cheeseburger. You could do that. You have someone come in every week to clean your apartment, right? Arnie says, Yeah, she comes on Monday. I say, She can clean the frying pan for you.

THE PARK

Leo is a carpenter who works for Arnie and Morey at the real estate office. Anna works in a kitchen at a local community center in her neighborhood. Their English is steadily improving, but when they're together they speak Polish, their native language. They both survived the Holocaust, but they don't dwell on it. Over time they've formed a bond that may lead to something serious, but for now both of them are trying to get a grip on their new lives, especially Anna. Leo has an apartment above the real estate office, and Anna lives with her niece and niece's husband. On Sunday when it's warm, Anna packs a picnic basket and she and Leo walk to the city park, as their families might have done in Europe during better times. They find a bench near the duck pond and watch the ducks. They make comments about everything—the ducks, the trees, the leaves, the sky, everything they see. There's a sense of calm and happiness in the park that pleases them. They sit and have lunch and watch children playing near the pond and the people passing by with their dogs. Anna sees a greyhound and says, Look Leo, such a beautiful dog. Leo says, Can you imagine the cost to feed such an animal? There's a slight breeze, and Leo says, Anna, you're cold, take my jacket. Anna says, No Leo, I'm fine. Leo says, Anna, you make good sandwiches but you hardly eat. Anna says, I'm slow, Leo. Leo says, Anna, do you like your job at the community center? Anna says, Yes, it's fine. Leo says, But you walk so far to work, I should drive you. Anna says, No, it's only four blocks to the center, Leo. I'm fine. I enjoy being alone, separate from everything. Leo says, Anna, do you understand the signs and the lights, when you come to a corner? Sure, Anna says. The big street with the light, I wait till it turns red, then I go. Leo says, Before you go, do you look both ways, Anna? Yes, I look to the sides, sure, Anna says. And you go on ladders. Leo says, Anna, it's easy for me. Anna says, Do you have good shoes? Sure, of course, Leo says. Anna says, During the war, we found a way to stay alive for so long when they hunted us, and now we worry about every little thing. Leo says, Let's watch the children, Anna. They behave like we used to. Anna says, Yes, we should be like them, better for us. Leo smiles, and says, Anna, let's take a walk. I want to show you something. They walk a little way through the grass and come to a big tree all by itself. Leo says, Anna, this tree is over two hundred years old. Anna says, It's beautiful. Why do you imagine it's still here? There's a pause, and Leo says, Maybe lucky, like us.

SIGNS

Morey comes into the real estate office. He says to Arnie, If it isn't one thing, it's another. Arnie says, What's up? Morey says, Leo's up. I gave him a job to do with the new sales and rental signs. Arnie says, So, he didn't do it? Morey says, No, he did it, but he can't spell. *Rental* is *runtle* and *sale* is *sel*. Arnie says, You got to write it down for him, Morey. He's a fast learner. That's an easy fix. Morey says, I didn't yell at him. I just walked away. Arnie says, That's good. You didn't yell at him. He doesn't need that. Morey says, He does a good job. He just can't spell. Arnie says, Morey, he's Polish. When you came over as a boy, could you write English? Morey says, No, but I was good with numbers. Arnie laughs and says, Speaking of numbers, how about going to the horse races with me on Saturday? Morey says, What, Sultz give you one of those ESP tips? Arnie says, Yeah, he's pretty good at it. Morey says, What, losing money? So what's the tip? Arnie says, Baby Face in the first. Morey says, Didn't you lose a bundle with Sultz a while back? Arnie says, Yeah, a little. Morey says, you're going to lose your shirt again with that ESP business. Arnie says, Sultz is very good on the first pick, then he falls apart for some reason. Morey says, No staying power, right. Arnie says, He thinks too much. He's good for one round, and they both laugh.

DINER

Arnie drives to the lakefront area by fields of grass and the old grain silos, no longer used. They're like monuments, he thinks. In the distance, there are a few warehouses. He drives by a vacant small diner, the kind with stools around a counter. He thinks he'd like to own it. It's on the narrow paved road linked to the city's inner belt, now off the beaten path. He's thinking seasonal, get somebody to work it, and with a take-out window. Why not? Other highway shacks start that way selling hot dogs and hamburgers.

Arnie and the guys are driving to Toronto on the weekend. He calls me and says, You want to go? I say, What's there? Arnie says, Nothing. I say, Sounds good. Moe and Barney are in the back seat. It's quiet for a while and then Barney says, How come a Canadian quart of milk is bigger than ours? Moe says, 'Cause it ain't a quart. Then Arnie talks about the diner idea near the silos. Moe says, It sounds like a good idea. Arnie says, I know, but I think the insurance is over the top. Moe says, How come? Arnie says, It's risky without neighbors, you know, being out there by itself. Barney says, Who needs neighbors?

We pass a young lady on the highway standing next to her car, looking at her back tire. There's at least one kid in the car. Moe says, I think she's got a flat. Pull over and back up. Moe goes out and says, You need help, lady? She says, Thanks, I did the jack part, I just can't loosen the lugs. Moe doesn't respond. He takes the tire wrench, loosens the lugs, pulls the flat off, and puts the spare on. Moe says to her, They put the lugs on with a power drill now, so they're tough to get off. You're all set, lady. She says, Can I give you a couple of dollars? Moe waves his hand, turns, and goes back to the car. She says, Thank you mister. Barney says, Did she give you something?

29

Moe says, No, would you take money for something like that? Barney says, No, and Moe says, Then why ask? Barney says, I was just asking. Moe groans and puts his head back on the seat, and closes his eyes. Arnie says, Hey Moe, you sick? Moe mumbles something. Barney says, I think he's sick. Arnie says, Okay, we'll do this another time. He turns the car around and heads back. Close to home, Arnie pulls into a roadside hot dog shack. He says, Moe, you want to get out and see how you feel? I say, Let him sleep, as long as he's sleeping. But then Moe gets out and walks over to the shack. He buys two hot dogs, french fries, and a drink. The guys are in line behind him. Moe turns to them and says, I think I needed something to eat. Barney says, Hunger pains, huh?

TREE FARM

Arnie drives east on US 20 for about ten miles for no particular reason. It's where he drove when he first got a license. He pulls into a service area, gets gas, goes to the john, buys a cup of coffee, and heads back. There's an acre of early tree growth with a For Sale sign along the road, with a number to call. He calls and goes back to look at it. The Christmas trees seem to be about four to six feet high. He estimates over a thousand of them. It's late November. He shells out sixteen hundred dollars, thinking it's a steal. He'll call Leo to manage the cutting and trucking. Small stores and independent sellers will jump at the prices. Arnie calls me. He wants to show me the lot and have lunch. We walk into the tree rows. Arnie says, Beautiful, huh? I say, Arnie, these aren't Christmas trees. He says, What do you mean? I say, They're not evergreens. Arnie says, What the hell you talking about? Look, they got needles, they got cones. I say, Yeah, but so do tamaracks, Arnie, and tamaracks drop their needles in the fall, and they're doing it right now. Arnie says, You got to be kidding, for crying out loud. We get in the car and drive back. Arnie's quiet for a while and then he says, I wonder if we can cut them up and sell them for, what do they call them, Yule logs?

BILLBOARD

Arnie calls. He says, Hey, let's go for a ride, I want to show you something. He picks me up and we drive to the edge of town and park in front of a billboard. He says, There it is, we rented a billboard for a year. I say, You rented a billboard? Arnie says, It's been stripped, and we're not going to use it for a few weeks until the new design comes out. It's all yours. You're the artist, do a painting or something. I say, Arnie, you got to be kidding. No, Arnie says, it's all yours. I say, Arnie, Whatever I do will be covered up in a few weeks, and anyway, my paintings are just works in progress. Arnie says, You have a habit of backing away. Just spell it out, world-famous works in progress, with an address and phone number. Make it big. I say, So then what? Arnie says, Look, it doesn't matter, just paint something that people notice. Paint your foot, who cares, but make your name cover the whole billboard. What matters is your name. Name leads to fame, that's the game, Arnie says, Like the name of the wise guy who put a sink in that art show. Now the guy's famous, and he made good. I say, I don't think it was a sink. It might have been a urinal. Arnie says, It doesn't matter, the guy's on easy street because everyone knows his name.

QUESTION

Moe says to Arnie, Let me ask you something. How do you know when you're really in love? Arnie says, What, you think you're in love? Moe says, That's what I'm asking you. Arnie says, I don't know, maybe you're in love when you want to be with someone for good, not just to get laid. Moe says, Yeah, maybe that's it. Arnie says, You talking about Judy? Moe says, Yes and no. Arnie says, What are you talking about? Moe says, Someone else. She works next door. We had lunch. Arnie says, What's wrong with Judy? You've been going with Judy for what, over a year, maybe. Moe says, Nothing's wrong with Judy. Arnie says, So what's going on? You haven't even dated the other one. Moe says, I know. We just happen to meet and share a table. She's friendly. Arnie says, What's the matter with you, Moe? You got a problem? Moe says, No, I ain't got a problem. Arnie says, Does Judy have a problem? Moe says, No, Judy doesn't have a problem. Arnie says, Wise up, Moe, or the whole thing is going to blow up in your face and you'll end up with nothing. Moe says, Yeah.

THE DOCTOR

Arnie's second cousin is a doctor with an art collection. He tells him about me. Arnie says, He wants to see your work. He's a big deal at the art museum. I say, What do you mean, big deal? Arnie says, I think he's on the board. We'll drive out on Friday afternoon. What do you think? I say, Thanks, I don't know, Arnie. Arnie says, Hey, this guy can put you on the map. I say, Yeah, okay.

I decide to bring three small oil paintings and three drawings. We arrive at the doctor's Tudor house with the big lawn and trees lining the driveway. I say to Arnie, Did you tell him I'm an art student? Arnie says, You can tell him what you want. Don't worry, just show him your work.

A maid opens the door and leads us down a hall into a living room. The doctor enters with a broad smile, and Arnie introduces me to his cousin, Herbert. Herbert says, I'll be with you in a minute. Meanwhile, Herbert says, there's a few paintings here you might enjoy looking at. He leaves. I walk around. Arnie sits in a soft armchair taking it all in. Arnie says, I should have been a doctor. It's a large room, with limited wall space, furniture, fireplace, and two large, heavily draped windows. Among all of this, I find three paintings. One is a scene of a fox hunt. The other two are portraits of Herbert and presumably his wife, commissioned by a local artist I've heard of. I look closely at the fox hunt painting again. Herbert returns and says, You are looking at a nineteenth-century British work by the artist John Goode. Do you know his work? I say, It looks familiar. Herbert says, This is the only John Goode fox hunt painting in this country. I say, I didn't know that. Herbert says, Oh yes, it's a fact.

Herbert says, So, you're an artist. What kind of work do you do? I lean the three small paintings against a chair, and spread the three drawings on the carpet. Herbert says, Is this some sort of experimentation you're doing? I say, I suppose you could say that. Herbert says, You're obviously picking up tips from those abstract artists. Is this the direction you want to go? I say, I think so. Herbert says, I appreciate your coming by, but I collect art that is more specific. I say, That's okay, and my guess is that your fox hunt painting by John Goode is a good facsimile. Surprised, Herbert says, Well, now you're not only an artist, but an expert on English painting. I gather up my work. Arnie says something to Herbert and we leave. I apologize to Arnie in the car. I say, I shouldn't have said anything. Arnie says, I barely know him, except to say hello. They say he's a good doctor, some sort of specialist. Arnie says, How did you know about the painting? I say, There's one in the museum just like it.

EXPLAIN

Barney and I are sitting in Joey's Diner having coffee. Barney says, Tell me something, you're from our neighborhood, how did you fall into art and things like that? I mean, our parents are pretty much the same kind of people. We grew up going to the same schools and places, and most of us end up working in the family business. You only went to high school, like us. Sure, some kid is a knockout with the violin, but that ain't you. I guess someone said you were good at art when you copied something. I say, Barney, I don't remember that happening, but it could happen that way. In school, some kids are told they have ability if they can draw, so they get serious about it. Barney says, what's so serious about it? I say, I don't know. I guess if you're spending a lot of time doing it, it could be a problem or it could lead to something positive. Barney says, So you got a backup plan if it all goes down the toilet? I say, Barney, it's a long road of trial and error. As you develop your skills, you start reading and learning names and places and so on, and you take it from there. Barney says, Take what from where? I say, You're storing up stuff. It takes a long time to develop. Barney says, Develop what? I say, A way of describing things. Barney says, You lost me. If everything you want to describe is already there, why do it over, unless you just want to copy it and get paid off? I say, Barney, That's where self-expression comes in. Maybe I can put it another way. Barney says, Don't bother. You got a cigarette?

HELL

Arnie drives up to the curb. Moe and Barney get in. They sit and talk for a while. Arnie says, I saw the movie *To Hell and Back* last night. It's a good one. You might want to take it in. Moe says, When you go to hell you ain't coming back. They all laugh. Arnie says, It's a figure of speech. Moe says, Yeah, I got it. Barney says, So what are you saying, there ain't no hell? Moe says, Barney, if someone tells you to go to hell, they're just ticked off, right? Barney says, Don't all the religions have heaven and hell in them? Arnie says, I'm not sure, Barney. Someone said Jews go somewhere in the middle. It begins with a P, maybe Providence. Moe says, Yeah, my sister Ellen has a big art book with pictures of heaven and hell in color, but there ain't no picture for the middle. The picture of hell is a lot of naked guys and gals jumping around. Some of the gals are even upside down. Barney says, No kidding. Arnie says, Yeah, I've seen that. You don't want to go there. Moe says, The picture of heaven has a lady playing a harp and people sitting around listening to her, you know, like a peaceful scene. Barney says, Hell sounds like a lot more fun. I think I'd rather go to hell and jump around with all those guys and gals than sit and listen to a lady playing a harp.

WILD

Arnie makes a bad investment in the stock market. He says to me, The broker is a crook, and by the way, he's a friend of yours. I ask him who it is, and he says, Charlie Mann. I say, We were in eighth grade together. Arnie says, You want to go horseback riding? I say, I've never done that. He says, You don't have to do anything, just hold on. The horse does everything, nothing to it. We drive out to the stables. They saddle up two horses. Right away, Arnie takes off at a gallop. Eventually I catch up to him. He's on the ground, on his back. His horse is just standing there. Arnie gets up slowly. He says he's okay. He thinks they gave him a wild horse, probably to break him in a little. They know me here, he says. We walk the horses back to the stable.

SATURDAY NIGHT

Most of the guys make it down to Joey's Diner on Saturday night, stand outside and shoot the breeze. Moe's cousin Marvin is singing like the Mills Brothers, "Across the alley from the Alamo lived a Pinto pony and a Navajo, who sang a sort of Indian Idaho to the people passing by." Moe says, It ain't "Idaho," it's "Hi-de-ho to the people passing by." Marvin says, I never heard of that. What's Hi-de-ho? Moe says, I don't know, maybe some kind of Indian greeting. Barney says, You guys eat yet? Arnie and Leo arrive and they find a booth. Moe says, So what's up? Arnie says, My cousin in Colorado wants me to go in with him. He's got some property near Aspen. He's thinking about putting in an airstrip for private planes. Marvin says, Ain't he the one who was going to buy a ranch and raise horses? Arnie says, Yeah, that's on the back burner. Moe says, What's he bugging you for? Arnie says, He's looking for backers. Leo says, What's backers? Arnie says, People with a lot of dough. Barney says, So how come he's asking you?

The next day the guys are waiting to play handball in the park. There are two courts. Barney says, I'm not going to wait for these slowpokes to finish their game. I got to help my old man this afternoon. Arnie says, Tie games are longer, seeing who can hang in there and win. Moe says, Leo brought a sandwich. Thinking ahead, huh, Leo? Leo says, Somebody want half a sandwich? Barney says, No, Leo, nobody wants your sandwich. Enjoy your sandwich. What's in it? Leo says, Pastrami on rye. Barney says, I could live on them. Moe says, I doubt it. If you were stuck on an island with nothing but pastrami and rye for a week, you'd be sick. Barney says, Try me. The guys laugh. Moe says, What could you eat for that long and not be sick of? Barney says, Maybe chili con carne. Arnie says, Knowing you, you'd be dead in a week.

MOE'S BIRTHDAY

Arnie calls. He says, We're going to the Chez Ami next Saturday night for Moe's birthday. With you it'll make four couples. I say, Arnie, I don't have a date. Arnie says, You can take Barney's sister. It's all right with her. I say, Arnie, I don't think so. Arnie says, Have you seen her lately? She's filled out nice. I say, Arnie, what are you talking about? I'm not interested in Barney's sister. Arnie says, How about that artsy broad you took out? I'll help you out, if that's the issue. I say, Arnie, I appreciate it, but I'm not big on places with cover charges and expensive drinks I never heard of. I'll wish Moe a happy birthday when I see him at Joey's Diner. Arnie says, They have a cover charge because they have big-time entertainers. I say, Who would that be? Arnie says, Like the guy you hear on the radio all the time, Bobby Michaels. I say, Arnie, I'd pay not to hear him. Arnie says, Hey, it'll give you a chance to wear the white suit coat I gave you. I say, Arnie, that suit coat is for a wedding, isn't it? Yeah, Arnie says, but it doesn't matter, it looks good on you. I say, Arnie, I'll wear it at your wedding. Arnie says, That ain't in the forecast. I say, Arnie, have a good time. See you at Joey's.

GAS STATION

Moe promises his niece, Bella, that he'll come to her class and talk about his occupation, but he forgets about it, and the day is rescheduled. Bella goes to the garage after school and says, Uncle Moe, you're not going to forget you're coming to my class Wednesday morning, are you? Moe says, No, I won't forget, Bella, I'll be there at nine. I'll bring something from the garage, I don't know what. Moe arrives at the school in slacks and a sport shirt with a bag of tools. The teacher greets Moe and thanks him for coming. Then she stands in front of her desk and says, Thank you, Mr. Stein, for coming to our class and telling us about your occupation. Moe gets up and says, Hi, kids. I have a gas station and garage on the corner of Page and Central. Aside from the gas, we do car repairs. If you got a question about it, you can raise your hand. A kid says, Does somebody help you? Moe says, Yeah, I got a guy inside for the engine items and the cash register and another guy who works with me in the garage. Sometimes he helps out with the gas pumps. A kid says, What do you do in the garage? Moe says, We do tune-ups and fix flats, mostly, and we also replace worn-out parts like fan belts, windshield wipers, and burned-out bulbs and stuff like that. A kid says, What's a fan belt for? Moe says, The fan belt is a belt around a fan that cools the water in the radiator so the engine doesn't overheat. A kid says, What's a tune-up? Moe says, A tune-up is looking at everything under the hood to see if it's okay, like checking the spark plugs and changing the motor oil. A kid says, Why do you call it a tune-up? Moe says, I don't know, maybe somebody thought a good engine was suppose to hum. A kid says, What's a spark plug? Moe says, A spark plug? I got one here in my bag to show you. It ignites the gas in the piston, and then the piston goes up and down real fast, like little explosions, except everything is sealed, and that turns the drive shaft and makes the wheels go forward. A kid says, Do you get dirty a lot? Moe says, Yeah, you get pretty dirty, because a lot of joints under the car are greased, and together with the dirt from the road you get it on you. You don't think about it. At the end of the day, all that stuff comes off with the goop we use. A kid says, What's goop? Moe says, Goop is soap that's soft so you can scoop it up with your fingers. A kid says, Do you have one of those things that lifts a car up? Moe says, A lift, yeah, we got one. A kid says, Did you have to go to a school to learn all that? Moe says, No, my uncle lived next door to us. He had a car that always needed something, so we worked on it a lot. Then I worked on other cars. With cars, you learn by working on them because you got to see it in the front and underneath. A kid says, Can we come to your garage to see what an engine looks like? Moe says, Sure, that's a good idea. Then maybe what I'm saying would make more sense. We'll use the lift, too, so you can look under the car. Saturday afternoon after three is the best time, it's slow then. A kid says, What's slow then? Moe says, The garage work. A kid says, If we get dirty can we use the goop? The kids laugh. Moe says, Sure. A kid says, What else you got in your bag, Mr. Stein? Moe says, Yeah, okay. Here's what we call a tire iron. It's just a big wrench with four extensions, like a wheel, so you can grip it easily and loosen the lugs on the tire. A kid says, What's a lug? Moe says, I'll show you when you come to the garage. The kids are quiet. The teacher gets up and says, Thank you, Mr. Stein, for coming to our class today, and the kids say, Thank you, Mr. Stein.

VOICE

Driving at night, Ezio Pinza is singing "Some Enchanted Evening" on the radio. Arnie and I are singing along. Arnie says, I love him. I say, Ditto. Arnie says, My friend Jane thinks I have a good singing voice. I say, Jane told you that? Yeah, Arnie says. I say, Why would she say a thing like that? She's your girlfriend, right? Arnie says, We were in high school together. I say, But you see her a lot. Arnie says, She lives on the same block, how can I not see her? I've taken her to the movies a couple times. She thinks I can develop as a professional singer. I say, How would she know that? Arnie says, She's in a choir. I say, So what are you, a tenor? Arnie says, I don't know what I am. I say, Arnie, I think she's making a pitch. Might be, Arnie says. I say, What do you know about her? What does she do? Arnie says, I don't know. She hangs out with her girlfriends. I know she likes antiques. I say, Antiques, oh boy. You know what antiques are? Arnie says, What? I say, Expensive doodads. It's supposed to be old and rare. I say, Arnie, That's not a good sign. Arnie says, I hear you. I say, Do you like the same things? Arnie says, She likes the Buick. I say, Well, there you go.

BARNEY'S SISTER

Barney is sitting on a couch watching TV in his sister's house. He says, I don't feel so hot. She says, What's the matter? He says, I got a pain in my chest. She says, It's probably gas. Take a tablet. He says, I don't like those tablets. She says, What did you have for lunch? He says, What I usually have, a jar of pickled herring and bread. She says, Drink a glass of milk. He says, I don't like milk. I had cream cheese on the bread. She says, Well, that isn't going to work. You drink milk for an acid stomach. He says, Who knows, maybe I'm checking out. She says, Don't make a big deal out of it. You ain't checking out. Have a glass of milk. Why do you eat pickled herring all the time? He says, 'Cause I like it, why else. She says, Well, it doesn't seem to like you. Okay, once in a while, but every day? Use your imagination, there's got to be a second choice. You don't have pickled herring at Joey's restaurant, do you? He says, He prepares everything there. I usually go for a cheeseburger and a soda. She says, He's probably got a nice tuna salad on the lunch menu. Try it, and eat slower. Chew your food good. You eat too fast. He says, What makes you think I eat too fast? She says, Barney, you're no stranger, I'm your sister. He says, You got any chocolate milk?

DONKEY

Barney goes to a spring horse auction and buys a donkey. He calls Moe and tells him about it. Moe says, What are you, nuts? What you going to do with a donkey? Barney says, I don't know. They brought it out to the ring and I had to have it. Moe says, Where is it? It's down at the junkyard, Barney says. Moe says, Your dad okay with that? Barney says, He hasn't seen it yet. It's way back in one of the sheds. Moe says, What do they eat? Barney says, I'm not sure. I know they like apples. I saw that in a movie. Moe says, You bought yourself a lot of trouble, my friend. Why did you do that? Barney says, The guy sitting next to me said what they don't sell goes for dog food. Then they brought the little donkey out and nobody bid on him, and it got to me. Moe says, Does the junkyard have grass? Barney says, Maybe there's some. There's a lot of fields out there. Moe says, Yeah, and they belong to somebody else. There's probably a law against having that type of animal even though you're on the edge of town. You'd better check it out. Barney says, Yeah. I'd better check it out. It shouldn't be a problem. It's no bigger than a Great Dane. Moe says, Size has nothing to do with it, Barney. It's not a dog or cat. Did you get papers with the sale? How old is it? Barney says, He's six years old and his name is Chuck. You got to see him, Moe. He's so beautiful and friendly. He rubbed his head on my chest. Moe says, What are you going to do with him, ride him to work? Barney says, I don't think so. I think I'm heavier than he is. Moe says, Call Arnie, he knows about those animal farms that people visit. They may take it off your hands. Meanwhile, my friend, your leisure time and money is going for bales of hay. Barney says, I'll take him for a walk after work. We got a small lot behind the junkyard. Moe says, Take a shovel with you.

ELASTICS

Uncle Jerry from Belle Undergarments in Buffalo calls Arnie, who's in New York for a few days. He says, Arnie, before you come back, go down to Elastics on Thirty-First Street and talk to Solly. The edges are coming out uneven. Their phones are tied up. Go down and see what's going on. Arnie goes down to see Solly. Solly says, Yeah, we found the problem with the first shipment. It's okay now. I talked to Jerry. We know Buffalo lost work time on the bad order, so we make it up with extra sets. It's beyond compensation. Nobody's perfect. Arnie says, Okay, Solly, take the rest of the day off, and they both laugh. Solly says, How's Dad? Fine, Arnie says. Solly says, Look, Arnie, it's their show, but when you get back, advise them to upgrade at least one line. Saks is going minimal with the ladies undergarments. Less is better now, Arnie. You got to keep up. The patterns are changing all the time now. Even the window dummies are changing. Arnie says, I hear you. Solly says, You know, Arnie, people are never satisfied. They look for the latest. One day it's this and the next day it's something else. Arnie says, But it makes everyone happy, right? Solly says, I'm happy in August. Arnie says, What's in August? Solly says, I get out of here. I fly to London for that festival, what do you call them, Gilbert and Solomon. I'm nuts about them. Arnie says, You're kidding. I think it's Sullivan, Solly. Gilbert and Sullivan. Solly says, For some reason, Arnie, they make me feel good. They make me laugh. The words, the music, and the costumes, it's wonderful to see. I'll stay a week, see the whole line. You should try it. Arnie says, And I took you for a klezmer guy. Solly says, Klezmer I can get here. Arnie says, Solly, you're something else. Which one wrote the words? Solly says, I think it was Gilbert, maybe the other one. I'll send you a postcard. Arnie says, Okay, take care, Solly. Arnie walks up to Forty-Second Street, buys a hot dog, a pickle, and a soda and drives back to Buffalo.

THE RIFLE

It's summer. Arnie and the guys are at the Canadian beach, sunbathing and tossing the ball around. Out of nowhere, a man comes up to Harold, one of the guys, points a gun at him, and kills him with a single shot to the head. The man is eventually convicted and sent to prison for twenty years to life, but ever since that horrible day, Arnie travels with a rifle in the trunk of his car. He knows it doesn't make any sense, but he wants it in the car, especially when he's traveling long distances. Within a year, he finds a rifle range and takes target practice. He enjoys it and returns to the rifle range almost every week. Eventually he meets guys who are hunters, and decides that the following fall he'll go on a group hunting trip to Wyoming, to hunt antelope.

Everything is arranged. When their plane lands, they're driven to a motel in Lander, and after breakfast the next morning, two jeeps take the eight hunters from Buffalo to a broad sagebrush plain where they hunker down and wait for the antelope to appear. Within an hour, antelope are grazing on the plain as they do every morning. In a few minutes, Arnie shoots an antelope, and feels a sense of accomplishment and camaraderie with the rest of the hunters, who all seem to have done well and are elated. The guide and a photographer walk out with each shooter to take a photograph of them with their kill. In the distance, some of the hunters are laughing and drinking beer. Arnie walks through the sagebrush and reaches the antelope he bagged. He bends over and looks at the antelope's head in disbelief. He looks up quickly and then down again, and says in a quiet voice, Oh my god, what did I do?

STEEL PLANT

It's an hour to the Lackawanna Steel plant. I take two buses. I set my alarm for 5 a.m. If I'm late, they deduct so much every minute. The plant area is like a city. I get off the bus at the strip mill gate, punch the clock, and walk to my work area. There are four of us in a slag pit gang. I work with three Polish guys who look like brothers. My first day, they look at me like, Who the hell are you? When you're new, you're an outsider until you're there a while. At the end of the shift, we're covered with soot, like coming out of a coal mine. I feel more part of the gang when we all look alike covered in soot. At the end of the day we stand in line and air-hose ourselves off so they'll let us on a city bus going home.

A strip mill must be the noisiest place in the world, with banging, reverberating sounds off the high metal roof, like cracking thunder. We slide down six feet into the slag pit along the cold smelting line that needs cleaning and pile the slag into heavy canvas sacks. Then we crawl out and rope it up to be hauled away by loaders that hoist the slag into railroad cars. We do this over and over.

The crew boss is an older man who inspects the smelting lines and yells instructions over all the noise. Every hour he walks down the half-mile line to check the other gangs until he's so small we can't see him. When the boss is gone, the three guys I work with sit against the wall for some quick shut-eye. They look up every so often to see if the boss is coming back. It takes four men to do this job, so I get the point. Nothing happens unless the boss is around. To these guys, goofing off is being smart. I go along with it.

Going home, there are usually too many boarding the buses. I walk back a block to another bus stop in front of a saloon, figuring I might get a seat. One time my crew boss is there, and sees me. He says, Hey, it's you. I half smile. He says, You want a boilermaker? I say, Sure. He doesn't know my name, and I'm surprised he knows who I am. We go into the saloon. There's loud talking and a jukebox playing. I'm thinking, do I really want a shot of whiskey with a beer chaser? But wow, it hits the spot. What a treat, especially on a hot day. I say, Thanks a lot, boss. The boss turns and looks at me. He says, See you tomorrow, and walks away.

Weeks go by. Every day is the same. The boss is on the line a short way away talking to a maintenance chief, and we're pulling slag out of the trench, and the three guys behind me let go of the hauling rope, and I slide on my stomach toward the trench. I let go of the rope near the edge of the pit. Someone hollers out, A man down! It echoes down the line. The boss turns to see what's going on. He calls for a stretcher. The three brothers look surprised and back off. When a gang wants you out, they find a way to dump you.

I'm in the plant doctor's office lying on his exam table with a sore back. The doctor says, I'm going to try to relieve the pressure in your lower back. While he's pressing and twisting, he says, You're not going to be working in the pits for a while. How did this happen? I say, Pulling slag, the three guys behind me let go of the rope. The doctor says, That's a serious accusation. Are you sure? We pride ourselves on our safety record. The report came back that you slipped. I say, Okay, to hell with it, I'm going back to art school in a couple of weeks anyway. The doctor says, Oh, you're an artist, too? I say, Yeah, that's my goal. The doctor says, Well, good

50

luck with that, and as a matter of fact I recently began doing art myself. Isn't that a coincidence? I bought a numbers set and follow the instructions. Have you tried it? I say, No, I haven't.

NEED

Arnie is looking at one of my paintings. He says, Let me ask you something. I can understand that you want to make paintings, but then what do you do with them if you can't sell them? Who's going to go for this kind of thing? I know it fills a need. Is that a good way of putting it? I say, Yeah, sure. Arnie says, You say the chance of being recognized is pretty rare, so you're actually a small-fry gambler. How does it go, if the tree falls and nobody knows it, then you're off the charts. You're not even in the waiting room. I say, Arnie, When you're working on a painting, you see the possibilities of making it better. It might carry over, and give you more confidence. Arnie says, I don't know. Maybe artists feel good working on their paintings, but when they're walking down the street, I'll bet they feel the same as everybody else.

HITCHHIKER

Arnie's driving back to Buffalo. It's a cold November day. He enjoys driving the state road through villages and open countryside noticing the changes along the way, the old and the new combined, like the changes in himself since he joined a real estate firm. He has mixed feelings about it, but he knows all this unexpected altered energy is what he confronts every day, so he's going to take it like he finds it. As he drives closer, he sees what he thinks is a young girl in a long coat, with her thumb in the air and a suitcase on the ground. He slows to a stop ahead of her, gets out of the car, and says, Where you going? She says, Buffalo, with a look of apprehension. He says, Where in Buffalo? She says, The university area, I have a sister there. He says, Okay, throw your bag in the back seat and sit up front. They get in the car and drive off. He's thinking she's fourteen or fifteen, maybe running away from home, and he shouldn't have picked her up. He can hear his Uncle Morey say, She saw you coming, dummy, and you took the bait. Arnie says to her, You travel this way often? She says, No, not often. Arnie says, You from Rochester? She says, Yes. Arnie says, I'm not going to ask you a lot of questions. The girl says, Okay. Arnie says, Do you hitchhike a lot? She says, No, not often. Arnie says, Well that's good. She says, Are you going to warn me about all the dangers? Arnie waits a few seconds and then says quietly, There's a good reason why someone would flag a car down, but a small young lady who decides to hitchhike could be walking into a trap. You're taking a big chance. I don't know percentages, but it happens. Some guy picks you up, pulls off the road, maybe into one of those quiet rest areas, and you're powerless. Let me ask you something. Do you have a gun in your overcoat pocket? The girl says, Yes. Arnie says, Well, maybe you'd get a shot off, but a minor carrying a gun is breaking the law, and you would probably end up in prison anyway. A clever lawyer could turn the tables on you, like it's all your fault, and you could be convicted of murder and attempted robbery even though that's not what happened. They sit quiet for a minute. The girl doesn't say anything. Arnie says, You get my point? The girl, looking down at her shoes, says, Yes. Arnie says, Do you really have a sister at the university? The girl says, Yes. Arnie says, Get rid of the gun. She says, It only fires caps. Arnie says, Well that's good. I think you wanted to save the bus fare, right? She says, Yes. They arrive at the university. Arnie says, You got enough money to get home? She says, Yes. Arnie looks at her and says, Please don't do this anymore. She says, I'm not. She gets out, retrieves her suitcase from the back seat, turns toward Arnie, and says, Thank you, mister, and waves.

SCHLEP

Schlep has a grocery store. He's Arnie's uncle on his mother's side. His real name is Sanford, but he walks like he's dragging a load, so everyone calls him Schlep, which he's grown to accept. He's a worrywart, laughs a lot, and tells jokes, all wrapped in one. Arnie comes by now and then. Schlep says, Arnie, where's my delivery boy? I sent him out a half hour ago with the wagon. Where the hell is he? Arnie says, Uncle Schlep, what's the special of the week? Schlep says, Onions. Arnie says, You're kidding. Schlep says, Yeah, I'm kidding. You know, Arnie, there was a day when an onion to a lot of people was as popular as an apple is today. Arnie says, Where, back in the old country? Schlep says, Bread, a little schmaltz, and an onion was a lunch back then. Arnie says, That's why they couldn't wait to get out, right? Who needs bad breath? and they both laugh. Schlep says, How's your mother, you still got the clothing store? Arnie says, Uncle Schlep, I want to ask you something. You got a warehouse with a separate entrance in the back full of empty boxes, doing nothing, and here, you got a gallon jar in your deli counter of the best homemade sour pickles in the world, at least to me. If people knew you specialized in pickles, they would come and buy those pickles, young pickles, old pickles, whatever. My friend Moe's uncle makes wooden barrels and there's plenty of cuke farms we can bargain with. This is a moneymaker, Uncle Schlep. Think about it. If you want to do labels and jars, I'll do all the arranging, and get a distributor. Your name will be on every jar. If you want me to go in with you, I'll take ten percent, if it's agreeable. What do you think? Schlep say, It's an idea. I'll have to think about it. Arnie says, It's a good idea. Your old recipe is a gold mine, Uncle Schlep. This is the land of hot dogs and hamburgers. You can't miss.

RACER

Arnie calls. He says, I bought a racing car. I say, A racing car?
Arnie says, Yeah, a midget racer. It's a racing classification.
You got to see it. I say, Where is it? Arnie says, I'll pick you
up. We go down to a garage. He pulls the tarp off. I say, Wow,
it's beautiful. Can you get in it? Arnie says, Sure, it's a small
racer, but the seating space is about the same as the bigger
ones. It has to be brought up to standard, otherwise it's fine. I
say, You mean a new engine? Arnie says, Maybe a rebuilt one.
I'll have Moe look at it. He knows when it comes to cars. I say,
Have you seen the tires? They look bald. Arnie says, I think
they're supposed to be. I'll check with Moe. I say, Arnie, you
might have jumped the gun with this one. Arnie says, Are you
kidding? Do you know what the body alone is worth? I say,
What are you going to do with it? Arnie says, There's an open
invitation at the speedway next season. If we can get it up to
snuff, I can pay it off with one win, and then more wins puts
you ahead. I say, You've been racing around for a long time,
so this might be ideal for you. Arnie says, I'm not racing it.
It takes an athlete. It's a tough, dirty routine. You know how
I feel about dirt. I say, Oh, yeah, you can't have dirt on you,
because of your skin thing. Arnie says, I need an athlete who
can drive, like yourself. I say, Arnie, get one of the guys. Barney would jump at it, and you got Moe for the mechanical
stuff. Arnie says, Yeah, Barney's a good driver, and Moe for
the mechanical stuff. I'll make them an offer. I say, Tell them
they'll make the sports page.

TITLES

Arnie calls. I say, What's up? Arnie says, My sister Laura wants to see your paintings. She's interested in a still life. You got any? I say, Yeah, I got a few. Arnie says, What the hell are they? I say, A still life? Arnie says, Yeah. I say, It's usually a painting with fruit or vegetables on a table, sometimes with a wine bottle next to it. Arnie says, That's a weird name for it. Why not call it fruit or vegetables with a wine bottle next to it? I say, I don't know, Arnie. I think it means living things that don't move. Arnie says, Sounds like our friend Barney. We both laugh. Arnie says, Look, Laura doesn't know what you do. I think she wants apples and oranges to look like apples and oranges. You got anything like that? I say, No, but I got bananas that look like bananas. I say, Arnie, You never know what people are going to like. Where did she hear about still life? Arnie says, She said one of Ernest Hemingway's novels. I say, Maybe *The Sun Also Rises*. Arnie says, What? I say, That's the title. Arnie says, Titles are weird, aren't they? I say, Yeah, lots of things are weird.

MOTEL

Arnie says, You ever been in a motel? I say, no, why? Arnie says, They're springing up along the highways they're building now. I say, Yeah, they're widening the roads. Arnie says, More than that, they're going around cities, not through them. That's where the motels are going up. I say, So you planning to go somewhere? Arnie says, Let me explain something. Leo's a bona fide carpenter now. We got a start-up thing called Motel Pictures we're going to patent. They're fancy picture frames you screw into the wall. Leo's going to make them. The motel people will love it. You know why? I say, No, tell me. Arnie says, Because people always steal stuff. This will be one step ahead of the competition. What do you think? I say, Sounds like a good idea. Arnie says, So you on board? I say, On board for what? Arnie says, To make a set of pictures, maybe four different scenes, like the seasons, that anyone would go for, you know, a cottage in the woods with a stream and stuff. Then we'll photograph them and make a lot of them. I say, Arnie, the guy for this is Joseph, the old man who cleans the rooms at the Y. That's the kind of work he did in Austria, before the war. Go down to maintenance, he'll be glad to show you his work. He's already got a whole storage area of what you're thinking. Arnie says, He sounds like the right guy for this. I say, Yeah, he's your man. Arnie says, I don't understand you. I give you a chance to cash in, and you back away. I say, Arnie, I don't do that sort of thing. Arnie says, Yeah, I should have figured.

REMEMBER

Arnie calls. He says, Look, you know about my interest in extrasensory perception. I've been dreaming a lot the last few days, and you keep popping in and out. I just want to warn you. I've been getting violent images, and it doesn't look good for you. I know you don't buy all this, looking into the future, and I hope I'm wrong, but I just think you should stay close to home for a day or so. I say, What did you see? Arnie says, You're with us guys at the beach, and a guy comes up to you and shoots you. You die instantly. I say, Arnie, that happened six years ago. It was Harold who was shot. Arnie says, Yeah, the guy had a gun and we all froze, and he killed Harold. I say, Arnie, the guy was nuts. You were much further back when the gun went off, and Harold was already gone. The guy's in jail for life. It was awful, but you got to put it behind you. You couldn't have saved him. Arnie says, I still think you should stay home for a day or two. I say, Okay, Arnie, but I got to go to work tonight. Arnie says, I'm serious.

BANANAS

It's 1920, aboard the British White Star liner *Olympic*, sister ship of the *Titanic*. Arnie's Russian father and grandfather are coming to America. They're on deck looking out to sea. Grandfather says, We left Southampton when? I'll be an old man by the time we get there. It makes me sick, this boat. Father says, Papa, you won't be an old man. It's not the boat, it's the waves. Grandfather says, They should go where there's no waves. Waves are no good. I know the first boat they made fell apart. Father says, Papa, it didn't fall apart. It hit an iceberg. Grandfather says, Sure, it hit a piece of ice and fell apart. What's the difference? Father says, The *Titanic* was a beautiful ship. Grandfather says, It could have been beautiful on the outside and cheap on the inside. You think they're going to tell you? Father says, You want to go down below and check it out? Grandfather says, I got nothing else to do. Father says, Papa, look at the people relaxing in their deck chairs with the blankets and the books, smiling, talking to each other. Do they look worried? A steward in a white jacket is carrying a tray of refreshments. He's distributing it among the passengers on deck. Father says to the steward, What do you have today? The steward says, Today it's bananas, sir. He gives Father two bananas, something they've never seen before. Grandfather says, What did he call it? Father says, bananas. Maybe it's for seasickness. They walk back to their cabin, put the two bananas on the table, sit down opposite each other, and stare at the bright long objects. Grandfather says, It looks like something from the jungle. Maybe you should go back to the deck and see what everyone is doing with it. Father says, It's got a hard point. Grandfather says, It's not exactly a point, but it's a point. Father takes a knife and cuts a banana in half. They stare at the inside. Father says, Maybe it's the outside you eat. Grandfather says, The inside looks like something from a bug. I wouldn't touch it with a pole. Father bites into the peel and says, No good. Grandfather says, Yesterday it was plums. Plums I like. Now we're stuck with this.

VENICE

I pull into a rest stop on the highway, turn off the engine, close my eyes, and fall asleep. I dream about Arnie. He's a real estate agent in Venice, Italy, sitting in a gondola with a couple from Texas, worth billions. I'm the gondolier, standing behind them, paddling the oar, as we go up one inlet and down another. The couple from Texas point out all the palaces they want to buy, and Arnie replies, Oh, yes, that's a good choice, and the Clemente, beautiful as well, and let me point out the Ruzzini, and the Doge's Palace, and there's more ahead near the Piazza San Marco. The wife says, Can we have these palaces shipped? They'll look so pretty in our new theme park. Better yet, the husband says, just send us the front ends of these places. We got the framing they'll fit right into, back home. Lot of them look a little worn around the edges, and we don't need all that extra, and they all laugh. This way, we'll get them faster, the husband says. Don't you agree? Arnie says, Sounds reasonable. Would next Thursday be too soon?

FUDGE

Uncle Morey has an empty building with storefronts in a good locale. He asks Arnie to make the fudge people in New York a proposition to open another store in Buffalo, no taxes, no rent for two years for ten percent of the profit. I say, Is that a good deal? Arnie says, Yeah, I think it is, but they don't need it even for five percent. They're two brothers probably satisfied with what they got. This could be a distraction for them, but on the other hand you never know, business likes to grow. I say, Arnie, expanding isn't always better. Arnie says, It may not be, but fudge is reliable and stays pretty much the same. I say, What do you mean? Arnie says, If an average company's food product is doing well, in six months the ingredients are probably going to change and you're not going to notice it, at least for a while. The profits outweigh the quality, that's the way it is. I say, What, they all do this? Arnie says, Not all, but a lot of them. Companies are always looking to save costs and increase profits no matter how well they're doing. Fudge is simple. It stays the same. You don't need designers and freezers. I say, So where's the big changes? Arnie says, Packaged foods, especially baked goods, cakes, pies, bread, stuff like that. They throw out more than they sell, but they still make good. Take bagels, if it's got a hole in the middle, it's a bagel, right? Even the people making them don't know what they started with, what their grandparents were making. I say, Maybe they think they got something better. Arnie says, What they don't know doesn't bother them. You know what I mean?

DREAM

They're having breakfast in a corner shop. Barney says to
Arnie, I had a bad dream last night. Arnie says, What's bad,
you lose your wallet? That's a bad dream. Getting pulled over
for speeding. That's a bad dream, especially when you're not
dreaming. Barney says, It was so real, like it was really happening. I'm in a hotel. I'm checking out soon. I leave the
room and go down to the lobby for a few minutes, maybe
to buy a newspaper. I'm not sure why. It's evening. I don't
know why I'm checking out in the evening, maybe I have a
plane to catch. I leave the hotel, walk a few steps, and turn
around. I look back toward the hotel marquee and wonder if
I'm looking at the hotel I'm staying at. I go in the hotel hoping it's the right one and take the elevator, but I can't remember the floor I'm on. I look down. I'm in my pajamas. I get
off the elevator and stand in the hall wondering what to do,
but I can't think of anything. Arnie says, Is that it? Barney
says, Yeah, that's it. Arnie says, So you got lost. Dreams are
that way. Forget it, you don't go anywhere anyway.

SALESMEN

Arnie's driving back to Buffalo from Toronto. He's got his headlights on. It's not quite daylight. He's driving a little faster than the train going south, parallel with the road he's on. This is old hat. There's a crossover track about ten miles down, and he wants to get over it first. To Arnie, it's something to do. He's in a cocky mood. He beats the train, no problem.

There's a sales job opening in south Buffalo. In his mind, he thinks he can sell anything. He enters the office. There're about twelve men sitting in three rows on folding chairs. He joins them. A tall heavy man wearing a suit and tie is standing in front of them. The tall heavy man says, Did any of you notice the car in front of the office as you came in? Get up and take a look. The men go to the window, look at the car, and then sit down. The man says, That's a Lincoln Continental. It's mine, and I got it selling Barry vacuum cleaners. Then he stares at everyone. He hands out a sheet of paper to each of them. It asks them to answer a series of questions, such as, "If you're sitting in an auditorium up front and then look back toward the rear and notice a woman standing there, would you go back and offer her your seat?" and "If you see an old man with a cane about to cross a street, would you take his arm and help him to the other side?" Most of the men that morning don't qualify as Barry salesmen. Only Arnie and two others know you wouldn't do those things. They are asked to return the next day to see a film, then go out with a salesman.

The next morning they watch a film about the tradition of Barry vacuum cleaners and what it means to its employees. Then some little guy who looks a little disheveled comes in and says to Arnie, You're with me. They go to a side door of the building and bring out a bunch of ten-pound frozen turkeys and throw them in the trunk of the salesman's car. This week, if anyone calls the office and agrees to a demonstration, they get a free turkey. Jim, the salesman, and Arnie take off. Jim stops at a gas station. When he comes out, he says, That's where I wash up. Arnie figures he sleeps in his car. They go to a neighborhood where all the new little houses look alike. Jim says, Most of these people work at the car plant, sometimes both of them. A hefty blond in black tights and high heels answers the door. She says, You got the turkey? Jim gives her a turkey. They go in and Jim hooks up the vacuum cleaner, while complimenting the lady on the appearance of her living room. He shows her all the parts and options to what Arnie begins to suspect is a white elephant. A little later the husband comes in and says, What the hell you want that for, and she says, It does lots, just watch it. You don't have to bend over. He says, It's a noisy son of a bitch. She says, I want it, and Jim makes the sale. She says to Jim, This turkey doesn't look like ten pounds to me, and Jim says, Arnie, go out to the car and bring the lady another turkey. Driving home, Arnie nixes working for them, but he's thinking about Jim the salesman, working his way up with the grit and smarts to tough it out.

SAUCE

Arnie and I drive to the Italian section for a spaghetti lunch. He says, You ever been down here? I say, No. Arnie says, This place is tops for spaghetti. They cook the sauce all day to bring out the flavors. It's the real thing. I say, What, cooking all day? Arnie says, The ingredients aren't thrown in all at once. They're added in a sequence at different stages of the boiling. Each ingredient matures at a different stage. I say, You sound like you know what you're talking about. We both laugh. We get down to the restaurant, but it isn't there any more. Arnie says, They must have moved. Let's get some Sicilian pizza. You ever had it? I say, No. Arnie says, You'll love it. We'll go to Pazo's.

Pazo's is packed. Arnie looks around and says, Grab the little table over there in the corner. I'll get the pizza. After ten minutes, Arnie comes back with a tray of drinks and two pizzas. He says, Dig in, enjoy. I look at the pizza and say, Arnie, what are those dark wormlike things on the sauce? Arnie says, I think they're anchovies. You ever heard of them? I say, No, I never did. Arnie says, It punches up the flavor. It's like adding horseradish or mustard to something. Dig in, you'll love it. I say, What exactly are they? Arnie says, To tell you the truth, I haven't the slightest idea. Look around, everybody's eating the same thing. It's probably a tangy mushroom. The tables are right up against each other. I catch the eye of a woman sitting to my left and say, Excuse me, do you know what anchovies are? She says, Sure, they're in the ocean. I think they're little bottom feeders. I say, What, they're alive? She says, Sure, alive, but not now.

A GOOD YEAR

It's September. Walking to Joey's Diner, Moe says to Barney, Yom Kippur's coming up. You going to temple? Barney says, I'll dress up, but I ain't going to temple. It's boring. All they do is pray. Moe chuckles and says, Well, that's why you go. You atone for your sins for the past year. Barney says, I ain't committed any sins, so what's the point of that? He knows it. Moe says, Who knows it? Barney says, The man upstairs. Maybe I'll take in a movie. Moe says, Are you going to fast? Barney says, Why should I? If I fast, it's like admitting guilt, when in fact I had a good year. Moe says, So you didn't do anything to anyone you wished you hadn't? In other words, you think you're perfect? Barney says, Yeah, as far as I know. Moe says, You must have screwed up somewhere. If you did, and you forgot about it, Barney, or you didn't realize you did, he knows it. You better believe he knows it, and then you're on his list. Barney says, What list? I never heard of that. You mean, he writes names down? Where's he going to get a pencil and paper to write names down? What do you take me for, a dummy? Moe says, He doesn't need pencil and paper. He stores it in his head. Barney says, How do you know that? Maybe he ain't got a head. Maybe he's shaped like a tree or a cloud. Moe says, Barney, your father's going to be looking around for you, that's for sure. Barney's quiet for a second and says, Yeah, my father. Well, I might stop in for a few minutes.

GO FIGURE

Morey calls Arnie from the real estate office. He says, Arnie, I wouldn't bother with those metal-slat window attachments we talked about. Arnie says, Morey, they're like outdoor shades and very attractive. People are going for them, especially in the better neighborhoods. Morey says, I saw one today. It's a lot of pieces. Arnie says, Yeah, Morey, but I see a lot of them going up. Morey says, I think it's a Johnny One Note, Arnie, not essential like having a window fan. Arnie says, Fake jewelry, huh? Morey says, Fake's okay, but I think we'd lose our pants. Arnie says, You know, Morey, people don't need a lot of stuff, but they want it. Morey says, Sure, if you have an extra buck, it burns a hole in your pocket. They got to spend it, even if they don't need it. Arnie says, Right now, people are going for that big pink bird you stick on a lawn. Morey says, You lost me. Arnie says, The pink flamingo bird on a rod you stick in the grass. They're everywhere. Go figure. Morey says, Yes, I've seen one. I know the wholesaler. I'll give you his address. If you go by there, bring a few dozen to the office.

GREENS

Arnie says, I know a restaurant that puts dandelion greens in everything they make. Sounds crazy, but the place is always packed. We drive down to the dandelion restaurant for lunch, find a table, and order hamburger plates. Arnie takes a bite and says, Not bad, huh? It's like a health food place. What did you think? I say, Good hamburger. He says, They draw you in with the dandelions. I say, What does it look like? Arnie says, I don't know. Did you see anything green in there? I say, Everything is brown, right? Arnie says, The catsup is red. I say, So where's the dandelion green? Arnie says, The relish. The mustard is green. It's probably in the mustard. Driving back, Arnie says, Every year I spray weed killer on them if I see them on my lawn. I say, What, dandelions? Arnie says, Yeah, it's a weed. I say, But it's a flower, too, right? Arnie says, Yeah, it's a flower until the flower falls off. Then it's a weed.

BARNEY

Arnie drives back to the real estate office after looking at a house along Lake Erie. He pulls into a turnout, gets out to stretch, and stares across a landscape of grape vines held up by row after row of fencing. He's thinking, generations of grape vines cultivated by generations of the same families. How lucky to be born in a setup like that. When he gets back to the real estate office, he learns that Barney left a note saying he was going to California.

For some reason, Barney drives to Los Angeles. He's there for a week and then drives back to Buffalo, so he's gone almost three weeks. His parents are delighted he's back home. His mom bakes him his favorite cake and his dad pours them both a whiskey in a shot glass, and says, Everybody needs to get away sometime. Later that evening, Barney meets up with the guys. They're whooping it up at Joey's Diner. Arnie gets there and says, Barney, how come you didn't tell us you were going to California? Moe says, He must've had a fight with the old man, huh? Joey, the owner, hollers across the counter, Go west, young man! Barney says, It was a spur-of-the-moment thing. Arnie says, What's it like in Los Angeles? Barney says, Lonely. The guys laugh.

FAVORITES

They're sitting in a booth and talking about their favorite foods. Arnie's trying to think of a name. He says, What's-his-name changed the way the world eats. Moe says, Who's what's-his-name? Arnie recalls and says, The peanut guy, Carver. God bless him. I can't do without his peanut butter. Barney says, I like peanut butter, those crackers with the cheese in it. Arnie says, Straight, Barney, you got to have it straight, without anything else in it. It'll keep you going without eating meat or fish. I keep a jar in the car just in case. Moe says, Yeah, just in case you're not having a steak sandwich at Joey's. Barney says, I know what I can't live without. What's that? Moe says. Barney says, Catsup. I can't do without it. Arnie says, What, catsup is a favorite food? You can do better than that. Barney says, Why should I do better? What good is a hamburger and french fries if you don't have catsup? Moe says, You got a point.

CARDS

Arnie calls. He says, You want to go to lunch? I say, I'd like to go by the old neighborhood and take some pictures today. Arnie says, I'll take you down. Be careful someone don't grab your camera and run. I got the rifle in the trunk. I say, Well, just leave it in the trunk. We get there, I take a few pictures, and we go to lunch. The next day Arnie phones. He says, Me and the guys are playing cards this Saturday, probably poker. You interested? I tell him, No, I don't play cards. Arnie says, What do you mean, you don't play cards? I say, I don't play cards, that's all. Arnie says, Why don't you play cards? I say, It doesn't interest me. Arnie says, well what do you do on Saturday night? I say, Nothing, maybe take in a movie or watch a ball game down at the playground. Arnie says, Look, we just play for nickels and dimes. What, are you broke? I say, I'm always broke. I just don't play cards. Arnie says, Do you fish? I say, Fish? Yeah, I fish. As a matter of fact, just when you called, I was pulling in a big tuna. Arnie says, Tuna to you, buddy. I'll call you next week.

LEO

Arnie drives around the suburbs, where new homes are being built. He's selling lawns, undercutting the competition by hauling in rolls of turf directly from the farms forty miles east of the city. Arnie has an aversion to dirt, even with gloves on. He attributes it to a skin disease. He hires Leo to do the physical work, as well as drive the truck. Leo's English is still limited, but he's content not to say much. Arnie assumes he doesn't like to converse. The war years have left their mark. Sometimes Arnie takes him to Joey's Diner at night, to be with the guys. Leo mostly shrugs or shakes his head when someone talks to him, as if he's sympathetic and understands. He often seems lost in thought, distant to everything, but no one fusses about him. It's when he's eating his hamburger that the past rushes in and his eyes sometimes tear up. He recalls the bugs and roots he ate to stay alive. Even if they see Leo's eyes, no one says anything. Sometimes he mutters, It's the onions.

GRADUATION

Barney drives the pie truck to Moe's gas station. He brings
sandwiches and drinks. They'll have lunch together in Moe's
office. Moe says, You got the sandwiches and drinks? Barney
says, Yeah, corned beef on rye and root beer. I got an extra
sandwich to split with you. Moe says, One is enough for me.
Barney says, Sometimes you want a little extra. It won't go
to waste. Moe says, It will go to your waist. Barney chuckles and says, I got coleslaw too. Moe says, You through delivering? Barney say, No, I got a few more stops. Moe says,
Hey, tell me, you ever going to finish up your last year of
high school and graduate? Barney says, No way, I ain't going
back there. I graduated to a better life. I like the job and they
like the way I'm doing it. That's good enough for me. Moe
says, They would have passed you if you hadn't skipped the
last few weeks. Barney says, My father needed help putting
up the new fence around the junkyard. Moe says, You had a
good excuse. You should have been in school. Barney says, I
didn't like their attitude. The teachers were always looking
down on you. Moe says, Yeah, they were looking down on
you, because they were standing and you were sitting. They
both laugh. Barney says, You need mustard? There's bags
of mustard here. Moe says, Yeah, I need mustard. Thanks.
Barney says, Aside from looking down on you, the second
thing is, they always wanted you to memorize stuff that had
nothing to do with you. Moe says, Barney, everything is new.
They're just trying to make you think about different experi-
ences. What are you going to do, drive the pie truck all your
life? Barney says, I like driving, and I'm my own boss, so to
speak. Moe says, You should think short term about that job,
Barney. Barney says, Why short term? Moe says, I'm saying
this as someone who grew up with you, Barney. You got
a man's job now, but you ain't graduated from those pies,

either. You're putting on weight. You keep eating those pies on the sly and you're going to have trouble getting in and out of the pie truck, or worse, maybe keel over one of these days. Barney says, Yeah, I got to graduate from these pies.

NATE

It's the first week in January. Arnie and Morey are in the real
estate office. Morey says, Arnie, do you need a new calendar
for your wall? Arnie says, No, I got a new one on my desk. I
borrowed one of Sultz's paintings for my wall. Hey, Morey,
maybe you'd like a painting on your wall. Morey says, With
all due respect, Arnie, I'm not a big fan of paintings. I know
they got big museums for that. I prefer my new truck calendar. Look at this Mack truck, Arnie. You ever drive something
like that? Arnie says, No, I haven't. Morey says, Arnie, enjoy
your painting. Arnie says, I will. Morey says, I'll tell you what
I enjoy, Arnie. When the weather's nice, on a Sunday, I walk
to the park, sit on a bench among all the trees, read the paper,
and watch the pigeons. That's my pleasure. That's enough for
me, Arnie. What I don't know, I don't miss. Arnie says, Morey,
you probably know more than you think. You've heard of the
Mona Lisa, haven't you? Morey says, Sure, the Mona Lisa
with the smile. Arnie says, Well, that's a start. You took notice
of a great painting. Morey says, What, are you kidding me?
It's on the radio all the time. What's his name, Nate sings it.
Arnie says, you mean Nat King Cole. Morey says, Yeah, him.
What a voice that man has.

AT THE Y

We go to the Y to play squash. It's my first time. I say to Arnie, Squash is a funny name for a game. What do we do, throw watermelons at each other? Arnie says, Where you been? It's an international sport. I say, I'm just kidding. We check out the rackets from the attendant, change clothes in the locker room, and hit the ball off the court walls for ten minutes. I say, Arnie, you want to keep score? Arnie says, No, we'll just practice until you get the hang of it. I'm thinking it's pretty simple, like handball with a racket. Arnie's getting winded. After a few minutes he says, My aunt's usually upstairs on Sunday, painting in the art room. Let's go up and see if she's there. Maybe you can give her a few tips. There's no class, but his aunt is upstairs alone, painting from a still life of small apples in a bowl and a wine bottle on a tablecloth. Arnie gives her a kiss on the cheek and says, Aunt Rae, this guy's a real artist. I say, Hello. Arnie says, Tell her what you think. I say, It looks like you don't need any help from me. You're doing just fine. Aunt Rae says, That's what the instructor keeps telling me, I'm doing just fine, and I know there must be something wrong, either with me or with him. Arnie says, Why? Aunt Rae says, Well if I'm doing just fine, how come I don't know it?

ROMAN

Morey says, Who's the carpenter Sultz knows? Arnie says, His name is Roman, a big Polish guy. He's good. He works with Sultz's father, the roofer, I think his name is Dave. Why, you need a carpenter? Morey says, Yeah, the church property we're handling needs some wall and roof repair. Arnie says, You ever handle a deal like this? Morey says, What's the difference? It's real estate. They're consolidating with a big church midtown and we're talking with the black Methodist group in the neighborhood. Morey says, Look, call his old man and tell him we'll need a carpenter as well, and we'll meet at the church when he's free. Arnie says, You know why they work together? Morey says, No. Arnie says, They both speak Polish and Roman ain't good at much else. They say he went into a crematorium and asked for a pint of cream. Morey laughs and says, That's a great story. Did it really happen? Arnie says, Yeah, a few years back. Sultz said he's been here over ten years, saving up, and planning to go back to Poland. Morey says, No kidding. Arnie says, I think he's got family back there and he's homesick. Morey says, He'll be the richest guy on the block.

TONTO

They get out of the movies. Barney says, You want to grab a bite? Moe says, Yeah, I'm hungry. Barney says, What else is new, and you slept through most of the movie. You might as well stay home. Moe says, Love stories are boring. The guy takes her home after a date and says, I had a wonderful night and all that mush. Who cares? I like the Saturday serials. I never sleep through them. Barney says, You talking about Flash Gordon or the Lone Ranger? They're for kids. Moe says, Where does it say that? Anyone can appreciate good drama. Anyway, kids are better judges of what holds your attention. I enjoy the Lone Ranger and Tonto talking to each other and all the action that follows. Barney says, You're kidding, you can memorize all the action that follows. It's always the same. They're on their horses. Lone Ranger says, "Tonto, let's go after those bad guys. You go that way and I'll circle around." And Tonto says "Kemosabe," which is probably Indian for "good idea." Moe says, The big difference is something always comes up. That's where the plot thickens. A rifle jams or something that puts them behind the eight ball. Barney says, But in the end the good guys always win. Moe says, Well yeah, that's what you're paying to see.

CAMPING WITH ARNIE

Arnie calls. He says, You want to go camping? We'll take fishing poles along. I say, Sure, when? He says, Look, remember the tent I bought in New York? Let's take it to the park and see if we can put it up. We drive to the city park, and spread it out on the grass. It's not a two-person tent. There's a lot of poles, and the canvas looks much bigger than normal, more like a house. Arnie is looking for the instructions. We manage to get it back in the box.

Arnie calls the following week. He says, I got a couple of sleeping bags. We'll sleep under the stars, like the pioneers. What do you say? You still want to go, I'll pick you up. I say, Sure. We drive for hours north of Toronto to Georgian Bay. I ask Arnie if he's ever been here before. He says, Yeah, it's all little islands. You'll love it.

We get to the dock late in the afternoon. Arnie rents a little boat with an outboard motor. We throw the gear into the boat and head off into the bay. By the time we reach a little island, it's getting close to sundown. We pull up on a sandbar and empty the boat—sleeping bags, candy bars, fishing poles, and a long dagger in a sheath, I guess for gutting the fish. I tell Arnie if he wants a cooking fire, I'll get some dry sticks. He says, I forgot the hot dogs and buns. Then we hear droning, like airplanes approaching, and it's a million mosquitoes. Arnie says, Oh my God, this is terrible. We crawl into the sleeping bags and cover our faces with our shirts and sweat it out through the night.

In the morning, we each have a candy bar and push off into the bay. A few minutes later, Arnie cuts the engine. It's a beautiful sight and total silence. I'm thinking this is where we're going to fish. I say to Arnie, Is this where we're going to fish? He says, No, we seem to have run out of gas. We float around for an hour until some guy in a boat comes along, throws us a rope, and pulls us into the dock. Arnie says, Sometimes nature doesn't cooperate. I don't say anything. I'm glad we're heading back.

FOOD

Arnie's Canadian cousin, Felix, has a landscaping business in Toronto with a city contract this year for public parks and boulevard care. Along with grass, bush, and tree trimming, they fill a truck with acorns from the city's Oak Tree Park. Felix wonders if they're worth anything. He calls Arnie. He says, Arnie, you want a dump truck full of acorns? Arnie says, Describe them. Felix says, Acorns, the nut that falls off oak trees. Arnie says, Felix, I don't know oak trees. Describe the thing. Felix says, It's got a little cap on it. Arnie says, I think I've seen them. Can you eat them? Felix says, I don't know. One of my drivers said Indians used it for something back in the old days, I think flour. I'm wondering if there's any commercial value in this, like fertilizer or something. Arnie says, I'll get back to you. Arnie checks around and calls Felix back. He says, Felix, It's considered a plant. You can't cross the bridge without a government permit. Why don't you check with, what do you call them, your First Nations office. Maybe they still use it. Felix says, Yeah, that's an idea.

Arnie and Moe are sitting in Joey's Diner. Moe says, Arnie, did you know that every day half the people in the world go hungry? Arnie says, So what are you going to do, Moe, stop eating? Moe says, No, I just heard it. Arnie says, Moe, it's nothing new. Moe says, Yesterday my aunt Sadie was talking about someone back in Russia she saw cooking a beaver hat to make soup stock. Arnie says, Moe, why all the interest in this? If you want to help feed someone who's hungry, make a donation to some organization, or ask somebody in the library about it, or call your state representative. Moe says, Call my representative, now who would that be? Arnie says, You know, Marvin what's-his-name. Moe says, Oh, him, he don't know nothing.

SKILL

I drive to Joey's Diner. The guys are sitting in a booth. Arnie says, You still got the Chevy with the bald tires? I say, Yeah, I drive it to art school. Moe says, How's the brakes? I say, Could be better. Moe says, Bring it by the garage, maybe I can do something. Arnie says, You got to have moolah, buddy, that's a fact of life. You ain't going to pick up any chicks in that car. You shouldn't be driving on bald tires. Barney says, It's a free country, right, as long as he's not breaking the law. If he wants to drive on bald tires, then so what? Arnie says, Barney, what are you talking about? I say, I think I'll go to New York, get a night job, and paint during the day, until I can figure out the next step. Barney chuckles and says, The next step could be the poorhouse. Moe says, Hey, Arnie, you don't have any particular skill, but you do all right. Sometimes it doesn't pan out, but a lot of it works for you. You see, Arnie can't do anything, but he does all right. Just do like Arnie. Arnie laughs. He says, Very funny, Moe. You know, a lot of people make a living using their brains, instead of their brawn. Barney says, What's brawn? Moe says, Muscles. Arnie says to Moe, You're good at repairing cars. Nothing wrong with that, except you'll never have clean hands, no matter how much soap you use. You can do all that, but with my skin condition, I don't have the freedom to do whatever I want. Barney says, What's a skin condition? Moe says, It means he doesn't want to get his hands dirty.

SYMPHONY

We're in Joey's. Arnie says, You free Tuesday night? We're all going to the races to see the fillies that ran in the Belmont. I say, No, I'm going to the symphony Tuesday night. Arnie says, you're going to the symphony? I say, Yeah, I'm going to the symphony. Arnie says, You and my old man. He's sold on that stuff. I say, You ever been? Arnie says, No. I say, You should try it sometime. It might surprise you. Arnie says, What'd it cost you? I say, A friend gave me his ticket. Arnie says, You should tag along with my old man. He'll buy your food and drink. I say, I'm not going there to eat. It's not a sporting event, although I think there's a wine bar at intermission. Arnie says, So what are they playing? I say, A Schubert overture and a symphony. Arnie says, What's the difference? I say, An overture is like an introduction, and a symphony is like a long story. Maybe it's a two-hour program. Arnie says, I'll take a rain check on that. I say, I think you'd like seeing a conductor and thirty or forty musicians sitting in front of you putting it all together. Arnie says, I'll stick to popular music. I say, Nothing wrong with that. I like them both, but classical music is very different. Arnie says, I think you like the fancy-schmancy formality of it all. I say, Well, it's more than a three-minute catchy tune with a bounce. Arnie says, Yeah, you told me, two hours long.

PIE TRUCK

Barney delivers pies to village stores east of the city. He leaves
the factory at daybreak, gets on the highway, makes a bad turn
on a narrow crossroad, and runs the truck almost on its side
into a ditch. The egg salad sandwich he was eating splatters
all over him. He falls to the side and takes a knock against his
right arm, like a punch. He crawls out the other side thinking
now he's going to lose his job when the boss hears of this, and
all those mini pies, broken up. He opens the back gate, picks
up a pineapple pie heaped off to the side that wasn't busted
too bad, slides it out of the wrapper and takes a bite. Out of
nowhere there's a cop car behind him with its lights blink-
ing. The officer approaches and says, You okay? Barney says,
Yeah, I'm okay, officer. I got to call the bakery and my friend
Moe for his tow truck. The officer says, I'll do all that. Give
me the numbers and your license and I'll write up my report.
Barney says, Thanks, officer. You want a pie? Nobody's going
to buy them now. I got apple, pineapple, and cherry. The officer says, Thanks, I'll take a pineapple. Barney hands the officer a pineapple pie. Another squad car pulls in and the officer
comes up to see what's happening. Bob, the first officer, says,
He's okay, Jim. Jim says, What's he carrying? Bob says, Pies.
Barney says, Officer Jim, would you like a pie? Have a pie.
We got apple, pineapple, and cherry. Jim says, Well, thank
you, I'll take cherry. Barney says, Here you go, officer. Officer
Bob notices Barney's sleeve is torn. He says, Did you hurt
your arm? I got a first aid kit in the car. Let me wrap it for you
until you get it looked at. Officer Bob looks back and says,
Jim, you got a school bus waiting behind your vehicle. Jim
is having another pie. He eats what's left of the pie and goes
back to the bus while Officer Bob wraps up Barney's arm. The
driver in the school bus yells, I think I can get around you.
The officer says, Hold on a while, there's three vehicles half

on the road and a tow truck on the way. The bus driver says, No problem, officer. If these kids are late, they got a good excuse. The kids are laughing and talking loud, happy to break the everyday routine. Officer Jim says to the bus driver, How many kids you got? The bus driver says, Twenty-seven. The officer goes back and says to Barney, You want to get rid of some of those pies? There's twenty-seven kids here and a bus driver. Barney says, Yeah, sure, I got some trays in the truck. The two officers carry trays of pies back to the bus. The kids get quiet like they can't believe what's happening. Officer Jim says, Hey, Bob, there's an ambulance idling behind the bus. The driver and two ambulance attendants rush toward the pie truck. Bob, the first officer, says to them, He might've broke his arm. He's the guy in the white overalls over there behind the truck eating a pie. As they approach, Barney says, My arm hurts, that's all. The ambulance aide handles Barney's arm gently and says, Nothing's broken, but you have a bad bruise. Give it a rest for a few days. The officer wrapped it up nicely for you. Barney says, Yeah, sorry you made a trip for nothing. The aide says, we respond to all off-road accidents, so no need to apologize. Barney says, You guys like pie? No charge. I got apple, pineapple, and cherry. The aide says, Free pie, well thanks. Barney gives each of them their choice of pie. When Moe arrives with the tow truck, everyone is eating pie. Moe says to Barney, You okay? Barney says, Yeah, I'm okay. Moe says, What you got here, a picnic? Barney says, Yeah, take some pies back with you. We can't sell them like this. Then Irwin, the boss, arrives. He says, You okay, Barney? Barney says, Yeah boss, I'm okay. I'm sorry, boss, I went off the road. We got a lot of broken pies. Irwin says, They said there would be days like this. What a mess. Maybe one of the soup kitchens or the Salvation Army will take them. They can break them up for a dessert dish. Barney says, You want a pie, boss? Irwin says, Yeah, get me an apple.

BENNY

Arnie calls and says, Hey, happy birthday. I didn't get you nothing. Just kidding. Look, you're going to New York, right? I want to take you down to Benny's men's store and buy you a blazer for your birthday. You can look like a dope when a coat doesn't fit right. I think you know Benny from the East Side, a damn good tailor. I say, Arnie, that's over the top. Anyway, I have a suit coat. Arnie says, It's called a blazer now. Yeah, I've seen your suit coat. I'll pick you up tomorrow at noon.

Benny takes his time with the measuring, brings out several samples and I decide on the color and the material. They get through with the fitting and Arnie says, let's get a sandwich. I say, Thanks for the gift. Arnie says, When you get to be a big-time artist, you can put me down as one of your supporters, whatever you call them. I say, Look Arnie, before I leave town, I'm going to the art museum to see an exhibit of modern French paintings. You want to take a look? Arnie says, Yeah, why not? I've never been there.

We drive down the following Wednesday and walk around looking at the paintings of Matisse, Picasso, Cézanne, Van Gogh, and others. Arnie says, Are these for sale? I say, No, just for looking at. We walk through the three adjoining galleries. Arnie says, The paintings are on the bright side, aren't they? I say, Yes they are, good point, Arnie. Arnie says, Let's walk around again. I want to look a little closer. We stop at each painting for a few seconds, and Arnie stops at a pool-table painting by Van Gogh. He says, I can relate to this one with the pool-hall guys and the dim lights. It's after work with some of the guys around, chewing the fat, chalking up, playing eight ball. This pool hall is nothing to rave about, but I think he caught the mood. What's his name? I say, Vincent van Gogh. Did you ever hear of him? Arnie says, Yeah, I saw the movie. He went nuts and killed himself, right? I say, Yeah, in the movie, he shot himself, but it's more than just that. Arnie says, What's more than that?

SHOES

Arnie loses a bundle on the stock market. The next day he buys an expensive pair of shoes, packs the car, and drives westward. When he was a kid, someone told him, probably one of his uncles, that you can tell a man's worth by the shoes he's wearing. After a few nights in worn-out motels, he sleeps in the car on the edge of the North Platte River, near Kearney, Nebraska. He awakes to a chilly April fog, and realizes he isn't alone. Far from it. There are people everywhere holding binoculars. He gets out of his car, and an old man standing there says good morning. Arnie says, What are we looking at this morning? The old man says, I've never seen this many sandhill cranes in the river bog. They look up in the sky, and the man says, There's so many, you'd think they'd bump into each other. There's a chorus of honking coming from everywhere. Arnie looks down into the wide riverbed below, where a hundred or so cranes feed and watch their young moving around. Arnie says, Those little ones like to run, don't they? The old man says, That's why they call them colts. When they get older, their moms teach them how to dance, so they can show off and find a mate. Arnie says, Who would believe this? He feels good inside. The old man says, Come back in November. You can bag one. They're pretty good eating. The old man's words surprise Arnie. He looks up in the sky at a flock of cranes circling overhead. He says, Nice talking to you, goes to his car, turns and waves to the old man, and heads back east.

BAKING

Moe says to his cousin Ellen, You still teaching the Wednesday night cooking class at the Y? Ellen says, It's a baking class. Moe says, We play basketball on Wednesday night. How come I never run into you? Ellen says, We're in the basement kitchen, Moe, maybe that's why. Moe says, Maybe I'll come by. I'm sort of interested in that. Ellen says, What, eating? You have to be enrolled in the class. Moe says, What do you bake? Ellen says, It goes nine weeks. Three sessions on breads, three on cookies, and three on cakes. Enrollment is ten dollars, so we can buy the ingredients. Moe says, You left out pies. Ellen says, We don't do pies. The fee wouldn't cover it. Maybe next year we'll do pies. Moe says, If you need a judge, I'm qualified. Ellen laughs and says, What makes you qualified? Moe says, I'm a good judge of what's good. Ellen says, The students don't compete against each other, and they take home what they make, Moe. Moe says, So what happens to the stuff you make? Ellen says, I take it home. My kids eat it. Moe says, I'll pop down after basketball and say hello. Ellen says, There's no stopping you, Moe. They both laugh.

ZOO

Anna and Leo are sitting on a bench near the duck pond, eating a picnic lunch. Leo says, Anna, Maybe after you would like to walk to the zoo on the other side of the park? Anna says, Sure, Leo, I'd like that. After sitting for a while they walk to the zoo area. They approach the large monkey cages where the monkeys are sitting on branches staring expressionless at the people passing by. They stand in front of the cages. A tear runs down Anna's cheek. She covers her face with her hands. Leo says, Anna, what's wrong? He puts his arm around her and they return to a park bench. Anna says, I'm fine, Leo. I'm fine. A minute later she says, That was us, Leo. The same look, the cages. It's not right, Leo. Leo says, No, Anna, it's not right.

CHAUTAUQUA

It's July. Arnie calls. He says, I'm going to Chautauqua tomorrow. Ever been there? I say, No. Arnie says, It's concerts and
lectures on a beautiful lake. I'll pick you up at ten. We drive
fifty miles or so west to a valley on a lake, with lecture halls
and private cottages. We get out of the car and walk to the
edge of the lake. There's a few sail boats in the distance, and
people sitting in lawn chairs. I ask Arnie about the events. He
says, You look at what's scheduled, and buy a ticket if you're
interested. Most of them are in the evening. I say, Why don't
we go down to the lake first, sit on one of those benches, and
I'll make a couple of boat sketches? Arnie says, Yeah, sure,
let's go down there. We find a bench and sit. I draw for a
while. Arnie says, You ever been sailing? I say, No. Arnie says,
Me neither. Arnie says, I want you to meet someone here. I
told her we'd drop by. We drive up one of the lanes to a pretty
cottage. A woman comes out, gives Arnie a hug, and hands
him a bag. Arnie calls me over and introduces me to his sister.
They talk for a while and we head out. I say, so what's in the
bag? Arnie says, She makes cookies. Here, help yourself. On
our way back, he pulls off onto a side road in front of a house.
Arnie says, I didn't call this guy, but let's see if he's home. I
owe him some money. A man steps off a porch. Arnie gets out
of the car. They laugh and talk for a few minutes. He shakes
hands with the guy and heads back to the car. I say, Who's
your friend? Arnie says, I took a few sessions with him. He's
a leading authority on extrasensory perception. I say, Well,
then he knew you were coming, right? Arnie laughs and says,
Yeah, he did. Arnie says, So what did you think of Chautauqua? I say, Yeah, it's something.

MRS. STEIN

Moe's mom, Mrs. Stein, feeds the guys who come over on Sunday morning after ten. It's not formal. She calls it a bite. The guys call it an early lunch. Mr. Stein is at the men's club on Sunday mornings. He'll come in later. The guys come by and sit at a long table and talk, like they do when they go to Joey's Diner. There's soda, coffee, and juice if they want. The food is on the table—potato salad, coleslaw, pastrami, bagels, sweet rolls—and hot oatmeal in the kitchen. There's Mrs. Stein's gefilte fish as well. She knows what they like. The guys hang around and talk for a couple of hours, sports, girls, cars, whatever. Mrs. Stein likes to see them sitting around her table, as if eating was the solution to any problem. Before leaving, Arnie says, Mrs. Stein, thanks again, you're a wonderful cook. Mrs. Stein says, I didn't cook. Arnie says, The gefilte fish and potato salad are yours, aren't they? Mrs. Stein says, Yes, the gefilte fish and potato salad are mine. Arnie says, Mrs. Stein, was your mother a good cook? Mrs. Stein says, To tell you the truth, Arnie, not many wives knew good from bad, then. Everything was made pretty much the same way. Barney says, You can't find this in restaurants. Mrs. Stein says, Oh yes, you can find it. Barney says, Not at our house. Mrs. Stein says, Barney, there's a reason. Barney says, What's the reason? Mrs. Stein says, In the old country, the girls watched in the kitchen, but they couldn't write, so they would forget how it's made. They had no recipes to look up. Some could remember, but others couldn't. My father taught me to write. I would remember and write it down, a little bit of this, a little bit of that, when to take out from the oven, when to put in. Barney says, I love your potato salad, Mrs. Stein. Mrs. Stein says, Have all you want, Barney. It's not for sale. Men always go back for more. I'll tell you a secret. Moe says, Mom, you got a secret? I didn't know you had secrets. Mrs. Stein says,

When we first came over from the old country, most of the fruit and vegetables we saw in the marketplace was like meeting someone for the first time. We didn't know a turnip from a squash.

BORIS

It's my last day serving meals in a Catskill Resort. The next morning, I lie on my cot in an employee cottage I share with Boris, a Russian. I hear a car horn. It's Arnie, up from his meeting in New York. I introduce him to Boris, an okay guy, who has a low voice and never smiles. Boris was a Soviet paratrooper who got shot up and survived. He got a medal. Arnie says, You ready to go? I say, Yeah, we got paid, we're ready to go. I say to Boris, You ready to go? Boris says, Yeah, I'm ready to go. Boris gets in the back seat. We get on the highway to Buffalo. Arnie says, Hey Sultz, you know anything about the environment? I say, You mean nature? Arnie says, Yeah, maybe. There's companies now that show businesses how to protect nature and still make a profit. I say, They pay them for that? Arnie says, Yeah, it's a new thing. Boris says, They killed all the birds in my country. Arnie says, Boris, you still have family in Russia? Boris says, No, all killed, like birds. We stop at the next rest area and get coffee. I give Boris my phone number before we drop him off in Syracuse. I say, Don't lose it. Stick it in your pocket. Arnie says, Boris, if you come to Buffalo, I'll help you find a job. Boris says, Thank you. As we approach Buffalo, we pass the flat green farms that grow sod. Arnie talks about sod for a while. A few days later I get a phone call from Syracuse. It's the police. They want some information. They found the body of a man with a gun and my phone number in his pocket, in a bird sanctuary near Syracuse.

TONY'S

For twenty dollars a month, Arnie works out at Tony's boxing gym on Friday night. He runs the track and punches the bag. The serious fighters spar in the ring, work on footwork, jabs, uppercuts, and overhands, with the trainers close at hand. They spar with each other when their ring time comes up. Pro managers and trainers sit around the ring, sip coffee, and talk about the matches and prospects. Arnie's hands are wrapped before a trainer puts his gloves on. He knows it's just an act, but he loves the ambience. If the odds are good, he bets ten dollars on a Friday night match. There's a food counter off to the side, and sometimes he has the special, a sandwich that tastes like spam on rye, with a Vernor's ginger ale.

He's allowed to bring a guest once a month, so I go with him. I get laced up and punch the bag for a while. Arnie introduces me to Mickey, one of the floor trainers. He watches me at the bag and says, Let me see your hands. He says, You're not so bad punching, but your hands are too brittle from the looks of them. I say, Okay, somebody else can fight Graziano. We laugh. Arnie says, Sultz, watch this kid in the ring. He might be unattached. It would be fun to promote one of these guys. I say, I think this is all Tony territory. Arnie says, Yeah, this goes with the territory.

CROSLEY

Arnie picks Moe up at his gas station. They drive a few miles out of town to the house of one of Moe's customers. He's selling Moe his old Crosley. Moe's happy. He's always wanted a Crosley. He drives back in it, and Arnie follows in his car. In a few minutes, Moe dozes off and ends up in a shallow ditch with high brush along the road. They both get out of their cars, and Arnie says, What's going on? Moe says, I dozed off for a second. Arnie says, Oh boy, what a guy. Now you can take it to your garage and work on it. Moe says, Can you believe it? I think it's just scratched a little. Arnie says, Moe, you always wanted a Crosley. If it's just scratched, you're getting a second chance. Moe says, It'll probably need a little touch-up, that's all. Arnie says, You're lucky. You could have been killed, or even worse, busted the transmission. Moe laughs and says, Yeah, I know.

CRANK

Moe's dog bites a customer at the gas station. The guy's wearing Levis, so the bite doesn't break the skin, but he's upset about it. Moe apologizes and gives the guy a free oil change and wheel balance. Later, Moe tells Arnie about it. Arnie says, You're going to go broke with that dog. He's big and untrained. Moe says, Crank is a nice dog. Arnie says, Yeah, he's nice to you. What kind of a dog is he? Moe says, I think he's mostly shepherd. He's from Barney's litter at the junkyard. Arnie says, He'll do it again, Moe. I would take him back to the junkyard. Why did you name him Crank? Moe says, He sleeps under my truck's crankshaft. Arnie says, I would take him back to Barney's junkyard. There he can be cranky all he wants. Moe says, Well, then I won't have a dog. That's no good. Maybe I can train him. Arnie says, What do you feed him? Moe says, I give him what I don't eat when I make supper, the liver and the innards and all that. Arnie says, Raw? Moe says, Yeah, he loves it. Arnie says, You shouldn't feed him raw meat. No wonder he bites people. Why don't you buy him a big sack of the dry stuff? Moe says, That stuff is expensive. Arnie says, Don't feed him raw, Moe, or Crank is going to bite again. Then you'll know what expensive means. You'll get fined, and the SPCA will do away with the dog. Moe, that dog isn't going to change until you do.

NORA

Barney's cousin Nora calls him. She says, Hi, Barney. Barney says, Hi, Nora, how you been? Nora says, I'm fine, Barney. I want a favor. Barney says, What's up? Nora says, My boyfriend Joe is going out next Saturday night with the guys. They're going to a college basketball game they were planning to see. I want you to escort me to a fundraiser at the Y. Would you do that for me? The event is for couples. Barney says, What are they raising money for? Nora says, It's for medical equipment and staff of some sort. Barney says, Are you still going with Joe? Nora says, Of course, Barney. Barney says, It doesn't sound like it. Nora says, Barney, they had tickets way before this came up, and Joe doesn't like Chinese food. Barney says, How come they're having Chinese? Nora says, The fundraiser is called "Chinese and Dance." You give what you want, five dollars or up. It's kosher catered, a lot of food, and dancing on the side. Barney says, If this is what I think it is, Joe should be taking you. I can eat about anything, but I ain't dressing up and going dancing. Did you tell Joe you were going to ask me to take you to this? Nora says, Barney, what are you talking about? You and I are cousins. Barney says, Yeah, so were Franklin and Eleanor. They both laugh. Nora says, Barney, they were like royalty. They could do what they wanted. Barney says, Nora, I don't like dancing, and besides, I'm not good at it. Nora says, I got news for you, Barney, no one is, at least around here. If you don't mind holding my hand, you just move your legs back and forth. Barney says, I wonder if they're having those meatball things in the pockets with the soy sauce? Nora says, Sure, everything. Dancing is secondary. We'll sit at a table with friends and eat. Barney says, Okay, just for an hour or two. Nora says, Great. It's this Saturday, Barney. You still have the Buick? Barney says, Yeah, and I got a suit coat too, but I ain't wearing a tie. Nora says, You're a doll. Pick me up at six.

KOSHER

Barney's having an egg salad sandwich at Joey's. Moe's waiting for his milkshake. He says, Barney, when you sit down, you don't have to say a thing. He knows exactly what you want. Barney says, I eat other stuff. Moe says, Yeah, desserts. He probably thinks you're kosher. Barney chuckles and says, Well maybe I am, for the most part. Moe says, No way, my friend, you're either kosher or you're not kosher. There's no in-between. Barney says, Arnie says there's ways of allowing you to eat non-kosher food without it being a sin. Moe says, When would that be? Barney says, When you're traveling, I think. Moe says, I don't think so. I think he made that up to suit himself. Barney says, So I'm not a hundred percent kosher. So what? Is that a sin? Moe says, Yeah, pork and certain parts of an animal are forbidden according to Jewish law, and you can't have milk products after eating meat right away, and before that, all the meat you're allowed to eat has to be blessed by a rabbi before it's sold. Barney says, What's the punishment if you're not strictly kosher? Moe says, I don't know, Barney. Barney says, Well, if it's a sin and there's no punishment, then it's no big deal, just an Old World custom. It was a good law when they didn't have refrigeration. Moe says, That's a good point, Barney, but you know what? It's still on the books. Lucky for you there's no hell like the Christians got. Barney says, So what do we have instead of hell? Moe says, I don't know, Barney. Maybe when the kosher folks see you coming, they turn their backs to you. Barney says, That's okay with me. There's probably more of us than them.

CAROL

Moe's cousin Sharon and her husband Allan want Moe to meet a friend of theirs who's also single. They reserve four picnic tables in the city park for the Fourth of July for a few neighborhood friends and folks they know from high school and the community center. Sharon calls Moe two weeks before the picnic and tells him about it, the food, the badminton, the horseshoes, the rental canoes, the card playing, and Carol. Moe says, What's that last thing you said? Sharon says, You know Carol Fine from high school, the one who went to nursing school? Moe says, Yeah, she sat behind Rudy, the girl with the big nose. Sharon says, Moe, the rest of her has caught up to the nose. She's very pretty and single. Moe says, Me and the guys are probably doing stuff on the Fourth. I think Arnie's getting baseball tickets. Sharon says, Moe, we want you to come. There's nothing arranged. You'll meet her and say hello, or whatever you want to say. Moe says, Are you a matchmaker? Sharon says, Moe, I didn't mention you, I swear. You'll both be there, that's all. If you hit it off, you can take it from there. Moe says, Sharon, I know you mean well. Look, I'll call you back in a few days. Sharon says, Okay. By the way, it's hot dogs, hamburgers, fried chicken, potato salad, coleslaw and drinks. Moe says, You're setting a trap, huh? Sharon says, Yep. Moe calls Sharon a couple days later. He says, Give me the time and place. I'll come by for a while. Sharon says, Wonderful. If that's all you're going to do is eat, then so be it. Moe says, No, I'll do something else, maybe horseshoes. Sharon says, You're a character, you know that? When Moe arrives, everything's in full swing. The food is laid out on a table, Allan is serving hot dogs, and there's lots of talk and laughter around the picnic tables. The kids are playing badminton and horseshoes. Sharon comes up to Moe and says, Come with me, I want you to meet some old

105

friends. I'll bring you a plate of chicken and everything else. She takes his hand and they walk through the grass to a picnic table. Sharon says to Joe, Beth, and Carol, Hey, you guys, I think you all went to school together, right? Here's Moe. Joe says, My gosh, Moe Stein, long time no see. How you doing? The gals smile and say something that Moe doesn't make out. Moe says, Yeah, time flies. Joe says, You remember Beth and Carol. Moe says, Yeah, you both had measles? The gals laugh. Beth says, No, that was Mary Jones and someone else. Carol says, I seem to recall that you were absent a lot. Moe says, Yeah, I hated the place. Joe says, Who didn't? Carol says, So you're a mechanic? Moe says, Yeah, I got a gas station. Sharon brings over a huge portion of everything for Moe. She says, Is cola okay? Moe says, Yeah, fine. Moe says, Did you all eat? They all say they did. Moe digs in. The three others get up from the table, smile, and Joe says, Enjoy your lunch, Moe, we'll see you after you've eaten. We'll meet you at the lake. Moe says, Yeah, see you later. Beth says, Come down to the boat dock when you're finished. We need two in each canoe. Moe says, They got life jackets? Joe says, Sure, Moe, they're required. Moe says, Good, I don't float good. I'll be down in a bit. Carol says, Take your time, Moe, enjoy your meal. Moe finishes and walks down to the lake. Carol is waiting. She says, You want to go out? Moe says, How about next Friday, take in a movie? Carol says, I meant canoeing. Moe says, I know what you meant. Yeah, sure.

MILLIE

Arnie's father, Bert, calls. He says, What are you doing? Arnie says, Nothing. Bert says, That sounds like you. Arnie says, Good one, Bert. Bert says, Listen, it's about Tuesday nights, Arnie. Your mother's gone wacky. I don't know. Arnie says, Okay, I'll take care of it. Later he calls Millie, his mother. He says, Mom, how many years have you been married? She says, I don't know, Arnie, do you want me to look it up? Arnie says, No, I don't want you to look it up. Mom, he goes downtown to the main library on Tuesday nights. She says, He goes where? What's he doing? Why does he go at night? Arnie says, Because he works during the day. Mom, listen, here's what it is. He goes to the library. He sits in a booth and puts on earphones, and listens to classical music for two hours. Millie says, Why does he do that? What's wrong with the radio? Arnie says, Nothing, mom. That's what he does, okay? You got your ladies' bridge night, and he's got his classical music. So all's well, Mom. Give him some slack. She says, Give him what? Arnie says, Give him a hug, mom.

TURF

I'm driving to New York with Arnie. We approach the Palisades cliffs, on the west side of the river, not too far from the city. I say, Arnie, this is where the kingbirds chase the crows. Arnie says, Say that again? I say, It's a small bird in this area that protects its nest from other birds, especially crows. You see them around here chasing crows away. It's like they're biting their butts. They're called kingbirds. Arnie says, How do you know that? I say, I read about it. Arnie says, You read about it? I say, Yeah, in a book. Arnie says, I'll watch for them. Hey, there's one now. He laughs and says, Just kidding. Arnie says, That's interesting, all of us creatures trying to protect our own turf. I'll tell you three areas that keep others out. I say, What's that? Arnie says, Garbage, street paving, and the numbers. The families control all that. You don't go there. They'll bite your butt, good.

TIMES SQUARE 1953

A couple days after I arrive in New York, I go to an employment agency in lower Manhattan. They think a brokerage firm might take me on. I don't sound like the Bowery Boys. I can speak softly, in sentences, and wear a nice blazer. They go on face value. I fit the image, but I know I'm in the wrong place. I don't know much about numbers and I'm not drawn to it. The next day I go to the state employment agency, and sit in a room on a folding chair with a lot of other people waiting to be interviewed. I take the first job offered, a four to midnight front service job at the Hotel Astor. I go to the Broadway and Forty-Fourth Street entrance, fill out some paperwork, get a locker key, punch in, get measured for uniform size, and look like I've been there for years.

The starter on the floor shows me the ropes. It's a combination job—carrying bags, operating the elevator, opening car doors, delivering messages—easy to figure after the first go-around. I'm a step or two away from dishwashing, the absolute lowest on the totem pole, but it doesn't bother me. The job is simple steps. Nobody working there says, You new here? The turnover for the job is so routine, no one gives a hoot about it. Being invisible at night is fine for now. It pays the rent. I'm somebody during the day when I'm painting. At night I'm a guy in a blue uniform in Times Square.

MEYER

It's my last night at Mel's place on West Fourteenth Street before I move into my own place. Mel's father Meyer is here for a convention. He's a furrier from Buffalo with his own business, a short heavyset man who smokes cigars. He has a quiet way of speaking. He says, Let's walk to supper. I know a good kosher restaurant on Mott Street. It's a long walk from West Fourteenth Street to the Lower East Side, but he doesn't seem to mind, so we walk. The three of us amble slowly south to Mott Street. Meyer stops once in a while to look in a store window, especially if there are fur coats on display. Mel talks about a book he's reading. When we finally get to the restaurant, a man who looks a little like Meyer greets us as we enter. We're early, or it's a slow night. He has a big white apron around his waist. Our table is already decked out with a white tablecloth, a bowl of bread, mostly rye and challah, a dish of sauerkraut, one with sour pickles, and a large bottle of seltzer with a metal handle and nozzle. Our meal comes. We enjoy a tasty plate of roast chicken with kasha and gravy and peas and a side dish of stewed apples. There's no talk, we just eat. For dessert, a piece of delicious yellow pound cake and coffee. Meyer picks up the tab. On our way back to Mel's place, Meyer lights up a cigar and we walk slowly, stopping a couple times to look in store widows at more fur coats. When we get to Mel's place, we're ready to hit the sack. There's no discussion. Mel pulls the folding bed out of the wall. It's a double, so we all sleep on our backs in our underwear, on an angle, toward Meyer on the left, because he's shorter, with our feet hanging a little over the side, as if we did this every day.

THE LIGHT

I find a furnished room on the second floor with a window facing the street. The toilet and shower are down the hall. I call Arnie and tell him what I found and give him my address. He says, Look, Sultz, I talked to my cousin Jerry. He's got a real estate agency down near Wall Street. He's agreed to see you. You'll make a good impression. I think you'll fit in. You're no dummy, right? Go down there and talk to him. I say, Arnie, I got to have a second-shift or night job if I'm going to paint during the day. Arnie says, Does your room come with electricity? I say, Yeah, but I got to have some natural light as well. I'm going to need more than a couple of seventy-five watt bulbs to paint. Arnie chuckles a little and says, Sultz, when are you going to see the light? I say, Arnie, I got to do this.

VINNIE

Vinnie works the Forty-Fifth Street elevator at the Astor. He comes up to me in the workers' cafeteria and says, Hi, I'm Vinnie. You're new here, right? I say, Yeah. He says, What's your days off? I say, Sunday, Monday, why? He says, You got a driver's license? I say, Yeah, what's up? Vinnie says, My friend has a car service. He needs a driver for a couple hours on Sunday. He pays a hundred bucks, minus my ten percent for me getting you in. It could be steady work. I say, What's the job? Vinnie says, Like I said, just driving. I say, How come you're asking me and not somebody else? Vinnie says, The job calls for a clean-looking guy with a blank expression. That's you. Look, I'm giving you first crack at it. If you don't want it, I'll get somebody else. What's the problem? I say, Where do I go? Vinnie says, You go to 240 West Twenty-Third Street. You get there at 8 a.m. this Sunday, and knock on the green door next to the deli. They give you the keys, the car, and the instructions. You get paid in cash when you return the car. I say, You better write that all down, I'm going to forget some of that. Vinnie says, You write it down, I don't have pencil and paper. I say, What's the event? Vinnie says, I told you, they'll tell you when you get there. I say, I don't know, Vinnie. Vinnie says, Okay, forget it, I'll get somebody else. I say, I was planning to meet a friend on Sunday. I'll let you know in a couple of hours.

I go to the locker room to put my uniform on. The bell captain comes up to me and says, I saw you talking to Vinnie in the cafeteria. You're new here, so I'm saying this once. Did he mention the car service? I say, Yeah. The bell captain looks down and quietly says, This is between you and me. Vinnie's been here a long time. He does his job well, but he can take you for a ride you might not want to take. I say, Thanks, Captain.

STAN

I call my friend Mel. We're both living in New York now. He says, I'll come up to your place sometime. I say, How about next Monday? It's my day off. There's a bakery nearby. I'll get a half cake for breakfast and a quart of milk. Mel says, Make it mocha. I'll be up about nine. He arrives. He says, The room looks familiar. I say, Yeah, like the little Van Gogh painting with the bed. Mel looks at the painting I'm working on. We finish the cake and milk and walk to the university he goes to on West Twelfth Street. Along the way, he talks about stars. He says, Many of the stars you see at night actually broke up millions of years ago. He lost me there, but I enjoy listening to him.

A few weeks later, Mel calls. He says, How's the painting going? I say, Okay, I'm working on another one. He says, Look, Sultz, I got a philosopher friend. His name is Stan. He's blind, and he wants to meet you and see your painting. I say, What do you mean, you want me to come down and talk to him? Mel says, No, can you bring a small painting? He can see with his mind. He'll explain it. I say, Yeah, sure. I bring the painting down to the school on Sunday and meet Stan. He's a big guy, like Mel. We talk for a while, and then Stan says, Can I see the painting? I say, Sure. We sit facing each other. He's got his hand on the surface of the painting, and I talk about it. He's looking up, above my head, with a half smile on his face.

STEW

Arnie's in New York for a meeting. Later in the day we meet up for dinner at Mel's apartment on West Fourteenth Street. Arnie's opening another discount ladies' apparel store in Buffalo. He says, It's a much better deal than the other store. Mel says, So what's different? Arnie says, It's twice as big and I'll have two store guards. Mel says, Double the trouble. Arnie says, It'll be okay for now. I'm working on a Colorado land deal. My cousin and I are planning to buy up some land out there. There's a lot of abandoned mining towns with a handful of old-timers in them who'll take a thousand dollars and walk away. They've never seen that much. It's a fact. Arnie and I are sitting at the table. It's a hot day. The place is typical for the price—one room, enough space for a table and chairs, a bed that folds out of the wall, and a space to the side for a little combo stove and half refrigerator. The bathroom and shower are in the hall. There's a back window that looks out on a piece of ground with a thin tree in it surrounded by high walls on four sides, like the tree is in a little room. Mel's fan is blowing warm air around. He's working on his master's degree in philosophy. In the summer when he gets back to the apartment, he strips down to his jockey underwear. He fills a big cook pot with two cans of Dinty Moore stew and adds a couple cans of beans. Arnie says, Didn't we have Dinty Moore the last time we were here? Mel says, Yeah, you liked it. Arnie says, I was being polite. Let's go out and get something. It's on me. Mel says, There's a good restaurant a block down if you like Mexican. We walk down West Fourteenth Street to the Mexican restaurant. There's a special for the day. It sounds good. We all get the special. Everyone is digging in. The dinner tastes pretty much like Dinty Moore with beans added, but it's cool here and there's no one in his underwear.

LUNCH

I meet Mel at the New School in Greenwich Village. We'll have lunch together. We go upstairs to the room with the so-called Commie mural. The school is feeling the pressure, so they cover it up. Mel turns the light on and pulls the curtain to the side. We sit down to talk for a while. Mel says, What do you think? Do you know Orozco's work? I say, Yeah, he's for real. He's good. Just then, a security guard comes in and says, Hey, this room is off-limits. We get up and Mel says, Okay, we're leaving. We walk out of the building. Mel says, This is supposed to be a free country. I say, Yeah, sure. So Mel, what's for lunch? Mel says, A school buddy of mine gave me these two lunch tickets to the Roma Bar in the Village. It's a new place. If you order a steak sandwich, they give you a free drink from the bar. It's a come-on. Mel wears thick glasses. He's trying to read the small print. I say, What kind of drink, Mel? He says, A corkscrew. Wait a minute, I got it wrong. I say, You mean screwdriver? Yeah, Mel says, a screwdriver. If you buy a steak sandwich, they give you a free screwdriver. I say, Mel, what the hell is a screwdriver? Sounds like a screw job to me. Mel says, Let's go to the Automat. I say, Good choice. We go to the Automat and buy tuna sandwiches. There's not a lot of money floating between us. We get some water and find a table. Mel brings a bowl of hot water to the table. I say, Mel, what's with the hot water? He says, The catsup is free here. You want tomato soup with your sandwich? I say, Yeah, good idea.

NEW YEAR'S EVE AT THE ASTOR

I work New Year's Eve. A little lady, maybe in her forties, approaches my elevator. She's staying at the hotel. I say, Good evening. There's no eye contact, but she half smiles. I take her up to the sixth floor and return to the lobby. Charlie, the starter on the floor, says, She swam the English Channel. I say, What? Charlie says, The little lady you just took up, she's the first woman to swim the English Channel. I say, You're kidding. Charlie says, I'm not kidding. I say, You'd never take her for an athlete. Charlie says, The world is full of surprises.

All night I say, Good evening and watch your step. It's the language on the elevators unless someone asks you something. The hotel manager comes over and says, No cops on the elevators tonight, they'll be freeloading. If they approach you, give me a heads-up or send them to me. There's a doctors' party on the tenth, a constant stream going up. Later, they start coming down, wobbly, singing and hanging onto each other. One of them is crying. I say, Watch your step, then I open the doors, and he falls on the floor. West Pointers are the same. They go up to their parties straight-backed and quiet, and come down singing, swaying, and sick. Well, what the hell, it's New Year's Eve. An actor, I can't think of his name, comes into the elevator like he's swimming in a pool. He plays a butler. What's his name? Around midnight, the owner of the hotel comes in, Mr. C. He's also the New York State boxing commissioner, tall, handsome, smartly dressed, could be sixty. I say, Good evening, sir. He goes up to his suite on the eighth floor and taps me on the shoulder as he leaves. His way of saying thanks. After work, I meet up with Vic, another elevator operator, and we grab a bite.

THE BOXER

Whether he wins or loses, Billy hits the hotel's night bar a couple days after a fight. He enters the lobby and walks past my elevator. I say, Congratulations, Billy. Billy says, Thanks, kid. You see the fight? I say, No, I heard it on the radio with what's-his-name, the blow-by-blow guy, Dunphy. Billy says, Yeah, Dunphy. I say, Billy, what did you catch him with? Billy says, A right hook. I caught him with a right hook. I say, You caught him early, Billy. Billy says, Yeah, I caught him early. You see Chico around? I say, No, not today, Billy. You supposed to meet him? Billy says, Yeah, I'm supposed to meet him. I say, A little late today, Billy. Billy says, Yeah, a little late. How come I don't see you at the gym no more? You used to punch the bag and skip rope. You should ask them to set you up for a round, see what you can do. They're always looking for sparring partners. I say, Yeah, Billy, I was thinking about it, but one of the corner men, the bald-headed guy, told me my hands were no good, too brittle or something. Billy says, Joey told you that? He don't know nothing. I'll talk to Angie. Look, if you see Chico, tell him I'm in the bar. I say, Okay, Billy, I'll tell him you're in the bar. Billy says, Thanks, kid.

NOËL

There's a young man, possibly an actor, on the elevator with Noël Coward, the British playwright. Mr. Coward has a small red flower in his lapel, likely an unfurled rose. His dark blue tie and white shirt complement his snug grey blazer. He's speaking quietly and rapidly to the young man about one of his plays, referring to a scene about something dark and passionate in a dispassionate manner. He seems amused. He injects a line from one of his comic songs, and then something about the delicacy of a tea set. The young man chuckles quietly. When the door opens they get off, and I punch *Lobby* and return the elevator to the main floor.

MODEL

Arnie's got a meeting at the dress factory in New York. Later that day he calls me and we meet for dinner. He says, The ladies' wear people are expanding into menswear. They'll need models for their suits and coats. They're going to do fittings and photos on Wednesday. Isn't that one of your days off at the hotel? I say, Yeah. Arnie says, This is good money, Sultz. You're an average presentable guy, I think. Why not give it a try? I say, Me, a model? Arnie says, If they like you it's six consecutive Wednesdays with the possibility of renewal. The word is out, Sultz, and there's going to be a long line of guys down there for six jobs next Wednesday.

I go down early on Wednesday to the factory on West Thirty-Second Street. There's a long line already at the door. At noon they give the rest of us standing in line a number and tell us to go to lunch and come back at one. I go to a fruit stand, buy an apple, and take a walk. When I get back, a guy calls my number and takes me into the tailor shop. There's no introduction. A little bald man wearing a vest and holding a tape measure says, What's your shoulder size? I say, I'm not sure. He measures me and says, You're no good, forty is too big. Thirty-eight is the limit for men's shoulders. Thirty-six is best. He hollers, Bring in the next one.

I walk up Tenth Avenue and pass a long line of men and women. I figure, a food kitchen or a drug clinic. I ask a guy in line what the line is for. He says, Blood. They give you five dollars for a pint. He says, It's more than other places. I ask him who's collecting it. He looks irritated and says, I don't know, but you can't jump in line, fella, you got to go to the end.

SOMETHING GOOD

Arnie goes to Joey's for lunch. The guys are sitting in a booth having hamburgers and soda pop, and talking about things not worth buying. Arnie joins them. Barney says, I'll tell you what's a lousy buy, it's the shoe heels they're making now. Moe says, What's wrong with them? Barney says, They wear out before you know it, and always on one side. Arnie says, Lose a little weight and they'll last longer. Moe says, That's a sign that you're walking like a duck. You should point your toes more. Barney says, I ain't doing that. Moe says, The big loser for me is tire retreads. Customers complain about them all the time. It's supposed to be a temporary fix but they drive them till the treads fall off. Arnie says, Stop selling them. Moe says, Yeah, sure. Barney says, The most worthless thing on the shelf today is toothpaste. Arnie says, What's wrong with toothpaste? Barney says, Who needs it? I got toothpicks. Moe says, Didn't you have a hygiene class in school? You're supposed to brush your teeth after you eat. Barney says, Yeah, sure, who does that? Arnie says, Think of something good, Barney. Enjoy your lunch. Barney says, Okay, something good. A great drink you can buy for your money is that orange pop, what's it called? It's even better than fresh oranges. Moe says, Soda pop is the best you can think of? Soda pop is better than a banana split? Barney looks at Moe and doesn't say anything. Moe says, You must be losing your mind. Barney says, I forgot about them.

YURI

Uncle Morey has a nice apartment with maid service once a week. A cousin from Russia, a generation younger, named Yuri, comes to stay with him until the displaced persons agency can locate extended family living in California. Meanwhile, Morey is happy to see him and help him if he can. Uncle Morey came to America as a young boy and remembers enough Russian to converse, and Yuri has enough English to get by. Yuri was wounded as a Soviet tank soldier defending Stalingrad, but he seems quite fit now. They meet at the airport and give each other a hug, and Morey says, Welcome to America, and Yuri says, Thank you. Yuri was conscripted into the army when he was still a boy, and was discharged four years later. He had little education or professional skills beyond soldiering. Following the war, Yuri lived in a displaced persons camp doing odd jobs, mostly for the elderly who had little strength to help themselves. Morey takes him to his apartment and shows him to a spare bedroom, and makes tea. They sit down opposite each other and stare at each other in disbelief. Morey says, What kind of work are you able to do? Yuri says, Kill with tank gun, and they both laugh. Russian humor, Morey says.

JOEL

Morey's cousin Joel is in the middle stages of dementia. Some days are better than others. He lives with his widowed sister, Dora. They're both in their mid-sixties. Morey drops by on Thursday afternoons after work, if the weather is nice, and takes Joel for a walk around the block. Joel had a men's clothing store for a long time, but never married. Dora gives him things to do, like taking the garbage out, but even then, she has to watch that he doesn't walk off somewhere. If he's not watching television, he's in his room folding his own clothes, as if he still has a men's clothing store, or he straightens up his closet. When Morey enters his bedroom, Joel is folding a dress shirt. Morey says, Hi, Joel, how's it going? You're folding a shirt, I see. Joel says, You can't sell a quality shirt like this if it's not correctly folded. These young guys today think that's all a salesman does, is talk. There's an art to it, like other things. Morey says, I agree, Joel. You're absolutely right. Joel, do you have time for a walk around the block today? I came over to take a walk with you. Joel says, Yeah, sure, we can take a walk. Whose idea was that? Morey says, Joel, we do it every week when I come over. Joel says, Morey usually stops by and takes me for a walk. Morey says, Yeah, Joel, I'm Morey, your cousin, who takes you for a walk. Joel says, What's the matter, you don't have a car? Morey says, Sure, Joel, but walking is better for us. Put your shoes on and we'll take a little walk for a while. Joel says, You live here? You seem to hang around a lot. Morey goes to the door and says in a loud voice, Dora, we're going for a walk. Dora yells from the kitchen, Okay, have a nice walk, you two. They leave the house and walk on the sidewalk to the first corner. Joel says, Morey, I remember you when you were a kid selling newspapers. Morey says, You're right, Joel. That's wonderful that you remember that. Do you remember when we played marbles in the dirt at the

123

playground? Joel says, Where the hell are we going? Morey says, We're going around the block, Joel. You like to exercise, don't you? Joel says, Sure, exercise is good for you. Let's go around the block. Morey says, Okay, Joel. Give me your arm. We'll walk together arm in arm around the block. Joel says, You're my cousin, aren't you? Morey says, Of course I am. Joel says, I love you, Morey. Morey says, I love you too, Joel. Joel says, Look at that bird over there. What's he doing? Morey says, Maybe he's looking for a worm. Joel says, Yeah, maybe he's looking for a worm.

LONGHOUSE

There's a property for sale west of Buffalo, near Lake Erie. It's listed as "historical-attractive." Arnie drives down to meet the seller, an elderly woman who greets him in her driveway. She's tall, slender, and soft-spoken. They walk around the outside of the house. She says, It was originally a Seneca meetinghouse that belonged to the tribe. My great-grandfather surveyed this section of the reservation for the state and they bequeathed the house and five acres to him as payment. Arnie says, Do you have a deed? She says, Yes I do, and she shows him the deed. She says, My husband passed away recently and I've decided to live with my daughter. With the land included I'm hoping it will sell for at least fifty thousand dollars. Arnie says, So what we have here is an updated nineteenth-century house on five acres that adjoins the Seneca reservation. She says, Well yes, and the property is legally ours. Would you like to come inside and look around? Arnie says, Thank you, I would. She says, It's really a modern home. We have electricity and a deep well that met our needs, and it gave my husband the incentive to modernize it. Arnie walks around the house writing in his pad and then says, It's a very attractive home, and you should have no trouble selling it. They walk around the outside of the house again and Arnie says, Thank you very much for your time. I have your phone number. I'll talk to my partner and I'll get back to you as soon as possible. Arnie drives back to the office in Buffalo. He gives Morey the rundown and the information on the deed. He says, The man was a good carpenter. It's not patchwork, and it sits on a nice piece of land. She wants fifty. I think it could sell for thirty-five. Morey says, Why don't we check with the tribal office in Salamanca, and get their fix and see what their records say, if anything. They could have a suit filed in court on it. Arnie says, It could be a religious place,

125

one of those, what do they call them, longhouses. They might be waiting for her to conk out and then file a claim on it. It's public knowledge they were screwed out of a lot of land that adjoins what they have left. Morey says, Who knows how far it originally extended? Arnie says, You're sitting on it. Morey laughs and says, Is that right? We should check it out. Could be a hot potato. Somebody could have made a private deal that worked then without the tribe's knowledge. Let's find out first if it's on the reservation. Arnie says, I'll call the Seneca office in Salamanca and get the details. Morey says, If they contest it, forget it. Some weeks later Arnie hears the Seneca tribe and the woman occupying the house have come to a settlement. She can remain on the site until her death, after which the five acres revert back to the tribe. The tribe has no interest in the house. Whether the house is moved to another location is for her to decide.

LOOPS

Arnie's in New York meeting with the ladies' garment people. I'll drive back to Buffalo with him, for my cousin's wedding. He calls and says, Hey, Sultz, I got two tickets at the meeting, for a Yankee–Tiger game this afternoon. You want to go? We'll hit the road after the game. I say, Sounds good, I've never been to Yankee Stadium. Arnie says, I can better that. I've never been to a professional ball game. I say, You're kidding. The seats are close to the field between third and home. Arnie buys hot dogs and soda pops, and we find our seats. By the middle of the third inning, Arnie says, You seen enough? I can't sit here anymore. I say, Yeah, sure. We head out to the parking lot. Arnie says, How long does that go on? I say, Nine innings. Arnie says, You can sprout roots sitting there. On our way to the highway, we pass carnival posters nailed to trees. Arnie heads for the carnival, in the town of Rye. He says, Let's check it out. You like carnivals? I say, Yeah, I like carnivals, sure. We walk around and look at various rides and colorful booths. Arnie stops at one of the booths. For a quarter, they give you eight loops to toss. If you get four of the eight loops on any of the six poles, about ten feet away, they give you a big teddy bear. After spending a dollar and getting nowhere, Arnie's smiling, but he's had enough. We walk around some more. Arnie says, I think they have a fan behind the curtain, on the side there, that blows the loops away from the poles. I wouldn't put it past them.

MOVIE STARS

Arnie's back from New York. The guys are in a booth at Joey's. Barney says, Hot weather makes me hungry. I think I'll have a corned beef on rye and potato salad. Arnie says, I'm the opposite. When it's hot, I eat less. Barney says, Hey, Arnie, when you go to New York, do you see famous people, like actors, walking around? Arnie says, You might, but you don't. You see thousands of faces you don't know from Adam. Sometimes you recognize somebody, but when you get closer it's somebody else. I saw Julius La Rosa once, the guy on the Arthur Godfrey show. I passed him on the street. Moe says, Did you get his autograph? Arnie says, No, what for? Barney says, It could be worth something. Arnie says, I don't think so. On the other hand, a Frank Sinatra autograph could get you some bucks. Moe says, What are you going to do, stand on a corner hollering, "Autograph for sale?" Arnie says, No, you take it to a reputable pawn shop. They know what's in demand. It's like when the post office screws up a stamp, if it's one in a million, it's considered rare, so somebody's going to want it. Barney says, Some rich nut, huh? Arnie says, No, it's just another money deal. Sultz sees famous people working at the hotel all the time. I saw him last week. He said Ed Begley was coming around. Barney says, Just think, Sultz is rubbing shoulders with movie stars. Moe says, Sounds like an interesting job. Arnie says, Yeah, Sultz gets to be near them because he's carrying their bags. He's not sitting around talking to Ed Begley. Barney says, I'd rather talk to Julius La Rosa. Moe says, How come? Barney says, I never heard of Ed Begley.

PILES

I'm in Buffalo for a few days. I rent a car at the train station and drive a couple miles down Broadway to Dad's roofing and tinsmith shop. He hasn't arrived yet, but he knows I'm here, so I sit on the concrete step next to the store's plate glass window. Dad arrives and gets out of the truck. I say, Hi, Dad. He says, You shouldn't sit on the step, you'll get piles. I laugh a little. I say, Dad, what the hell are piles? Dad says, I don't know, but you don't want them. I say, You used to tell me that when I was a kid. Have you ever met anyone with piles? Dad says, Did you rent that car? I say, Yeah. Dad says, A waste of money. I could have picked you up. I say, Dad, you going drive me around in your pickup all day? Don't worry about it, I'm working. Dad says, What, the hotel job in Times Square? I say, Yeah, for the time being. I brought you a present for the house. I give Dad a little package. He opens it up and looks at it. He says, What is it? I say, Are you kidding? It's the good luck charm, a mezuzah you attach by the front door. I bought it in a religious article store. Dad says, Thanks, son, it's nice. I'll put it up at the entrance to the shop. What did it cost you? I say, Fifteen dollars. It's carved wood, one of a kind. Dad says, They saw you coming. Look, as long as you're down here, we'll stop by for a few minutes and say hello to your grandmother. I say, Great idea. She used to make spaghetti for us kids on Sundays. Did you tell her we were coming? Dad says, You don't need an invitation. We'll get her a Jewish newspaper on the way. I say, Has she learned any English yet? Dad says, No, they all speak Yiddish in my sister's house. She doesn't go anywhere, so she doesn't need it. If you listen, you'll understand what she's saying. I say, Dad, I can pick up what she's saying, but I'm not going to have a conversation with her. Dad says, When you were small you could. It doesn't matter. She'll be happy to see you. I say, Dad, when we stop for the newspaper, buy some hard candy. She likes hard candy. Dad says, you're right. You remembered that. I say, Yeah, candy I remember.

WEST

Arnie's in New York. We walk down Eighth Street in the Village. I have a job in the Village library, stacking books and reading stories to children. Arnie says, Is this temporary? I say, I think so. Arnie says, What are you reading today? I say, I'm not sure. I'll decide when I get there. Arnie says, Look, I know these two brothers, one's in New York, and the other is in San Francisco. They own an import car business. They transfer cars from coast to coast, coming from Europe or Japan. They hire drivers both ways. What do you think? Arnie says, Live it up for awhile. You get an expense account, and a decent salary to travel and see the sites in a new car. I say, Arnie, it sounds like a job for you. Arnie says, Yeah, but right now I'm busy with other stuff. I say, Arnie, I can't do it. Arnie says, Why not? I say, I'd be a wreck sitting in a car day after day. Arnie says, What are you talking about? These are new cars, not the piece of junk you were driving. I say, I know, Arnie, but for long distance, my back takes a square truck seat. If they were trucks, I'd consider it. Truck seats are made for that kind of life. Arnie says, I'll ask them if they ship trucks.

Arnie says, If I wasn't tied up right now, I'd go west myself, visit my cousin Lenny with the drug store in Aspen. He keeps asking me to come out. All his savings are tied up in land purchases. He's doing the right thing. I say, Like what? Arnie says, The mountains are a great drawing card. Living in Colorado year-round is catching on. Even if you only walk to the corner, you want to be there. You can play cowboy in the summer and go skiing in the winter. I say, If he keeps asking you to come out, why don't you give it a try? Arnie says, He has a lot of land, I could go in with him. We could hire a couple guys and raise quarter horses. Everyone out there wants a horse. It's an industry, with all those dude ranches. I say, Arnie, if you buy a cowboy hat and raise horses, I guess you're a cowboy. Arnie says, I got to do this.

MINI

Sol, from the ladies' wear factory in New York, calls Arnie about a new line. Arnie says, Sol, what you got? Sol says, It's a short dress or skirt above the knees, they're calling it a mini. It's taking off big-time. Jake says they're selling fast. We'll have four lots to go by next Tuesday. Arnie says, What are you doing, Sol, cutting everybody short? Sol laughs and says, We got new patterns too, Arnie. Can you set up for the summer? Arnie says, Yeah, Sol, we got the storefronts. Sol says, Good, we'll work out the percentages. Arnie says, Okay, I'll call Jerry and get back to you. Sol says, Do you still have a man here for the truck? Arnie says, Yeah, I'll call Sultz and see if he's available. Arnie calls me with the details. I say, Okay, the same warehouse on West Thirty-Third, Tuesday morning at seven. Arnie says, Sultz, when you get here, you can paint new store signs for us. I say, Arnie, I don't do signs. Arnie says, Yeah, I forgot. I'll get Leo.

MEL

It's summer. Mel's in Buffalo for a few weeks. He's sitting in a street-corner park with a book in his lap, waiting for Arnie, five minutes from his parents' house, the block he and Arnie grew up on. They spent much of those early years trying to outwit each other with silly, sometimes wicked pranks that seemed hilarious and fun to them, depending on who came out on top. Getting locked in a room or a car or a garage for an hour seemed to be a favorite. Arnie walks up and says, Hey, you're reading a book. Mel says, You find that unusual? Arnie says, Not for you. You still in school? Mel says, As a matter of fact, I am. Arnie says, Mel, how many years does it take to get a master's degree in psychology or whatever you're majoring in? Mel says, I have to write a dissertation. Arnie says, Well, write it and get out of that fleabag flat you live in. Mel says, I think you've stayed in that fleabag flat a couple times. Arnie says, Yeah, how can I forget it? Look, you want to meet up later on? The guys are going to that traveling carnival tonight on the edge of town, lots of animals and games. You want to go? Mel says, You going to eat first? Arnie says, There's plenty of food there, everything, hot dogs, hamburgers, ice cream, whatever you want. Mel says, Okay, pick me up at the house. Arnie says, I'll be there at four.

Later, Arnie comes by to pick up Mel. Mel says, I tried calling you, but you already left. Arnie says, What, you're not going? Mel says, I promised my Uncle Hymie we'd go to the movies tonight. Arnie says, I thought you were hungry for carnival food? Mel says, We're going to the ice cream shop after the movies. They have the special tonight. Arnie says, Oh, I get it. You're falling for that dumb Saturday night special. What is it? Mel says, If you finish two banana splits, you get the third one free. Arnie says, You're crazy, Mel. It's a come-on. They're selling you two banana splits. What's your uncle going to do, carry you home? You're not going to finish three banana splits. Mel says, Are you kidding me?

LISA

Morey's granddaughter Lisa is in the fifth grade. She goes to the real estate office to see him. She says, Hi, Grandpa. Morey says, Hi, sweetheart. You look so nice. Lisa says, Thank you, can I ask you a favor? Morey says, Sure what is it? Lisa says, Can you talk to my class about what you do? Morey says, Talk to your class? No, darling. I don't do those things. Lisa says, Why not, Grandpa? You taught Uncle Arnie and other people things. Morey says, Real estate is nothing to talk about. I show people some property and figure out the numbers, that's it. Lisa says, Grandpa, that's good, you can tell everybody about that. Morey says, There's not much to tell. I'll put everyone to sleep. It's a boring subject. Lisa, you should ask Sultz, he's in town for a few weeks. Arnie will call him and ask him if he'll do it. Lisa says, Sultz is an artist, isn't he? What's his profession? Morey says, I don't know, to him it's serious business.

I agree to talk to Lisa's class. I show up a week later, and Lisa's teacher says to the class, Mr. Sultz is our guest today. He is going to talk to you about being an artist. Thank you, Mr. Sultz, for coming to our class. I give the teacher a nod, and say to the class, Why don't we start out with a question? Just raise your hand if you have one. A student says, What kind of art do you do? I say, I paint mostly landscapes. A student says, What's a landscape? I say, It's a section of land, you know, like a big view. A student says, Do you have a store where you sell your work? I say, No, I have an apartment where I work. A student says, I heard that some paintings are worth millions of dollars. What's yours worth? I say, A lot less. I'm just starting out. A student says, Are you, like, a starving artist? I say, No, I'm not starving. I have a job. A student says, My big sister does that too. She works in a drug store all day, and at night she draws pictures of movie stars from magazines. A student says, How come artists are supposed to be so special? They didn't invent anything. I say, Well, no, they didn't invent anything. A student says, If artists are real good, do they get to be in a movie? I say, Well, no, not as a rule. A student says, Do artists go crazy because no one buys anything? I say, Well, I don't know about going crazy. A student says, My dad says artists are a bunch of homos. I say, Well, there's . . . The teacher quickly rises from her chair and says, Unfortunately, our visiting time is a little shorter today because of another event. A student says, Miss Brown, what other event? Miss Brown says, Class, let's thank Mr. Sultz for coming today. The class says, Thank you, Mr. Sultz.

PONCHOS

Solly from Elastics in New York calls Arnie. He says, How you doing, kid? Arnie says, Hey, what's cooking, Solly? Solly says, We just heard from the DOD, first time since the wool glove contract. Arnie says, Department of Defense, right? Solly says, Yeah, they want five hundred ponchos in Arizona by next April. Can you give me a long-haul driver? They're going to double-check his politics, everything, just so you know. He'll make a couple thousand for the delivery. If he wants, he can watch with the troops if he passes clearance. Arnie says, Watch what? Solly says, They're going to blow up another bomb, what do you call it, atom. They'll have front-row seats. I wish I could go. That would be something to see. Arnie says, So what's with the ponchos? They expecting rain? Solly laughs and says, The ponchos are made special for the event. They'll have elastic around the openings with whatever else they'll be wearing. Arnie says, Solly, the word is out on these bombs. They're radioactive. If you're exposed, you're going to get cancer. The poncho will be window dressing. You'll need a lead suit to be safe. Solly says, Arnie, who told you this? Arnie says, I read about it. Solly says, You read about it. Do you think the government is going to put our own soldiers in harm's way and expose them to cancer? Arnie says, Solly, I'm glad you're not going.

OFFICE TALK

Arnie and Morey are sitting in the office. Morey says, Business could be better, but the suburbs are strong. We shouldn't complain. Arnie says, You been down to Broadway lately? It's like a ghost town. Morey says, Funny thing, even during the Depression, the old neighborhoods held together. You didn't have a lot, but you had enough. Arnie says, You didn't know any better. They laugh. Morey says, When factories move out, the restaurants go bust and the neighborhood goes downhill. Arnie says, If somebody can make it cheaper, you're out of business, kaput. Here today, gone tomorrow. Morey says, Arnie, I'm staying where I am. Arnie laughs, and says, Yeah, me too, Morey.

Morey says, My cousin Sammy is going down to Florida for a month. It's getting popular, people going down there. Arnie says, Cars are pretty reliable now. They can take their time and see the country. Morey says, Better yet, they can fly down. Arnie says, You been down there? Morey says, No I haven't, Arnie, I read an article. Maybe someday I'll give it a try. Arnie says, I don't know, there's something weird about it. It's so different. Morey says, Yeah, like the weather. They laugh. Morey says, The old guys walk the ocean boardwalks like beach bums with their sandals and shorts, and get roasted. Arnie says, Self-inflicted pain. Morey says, People like warm sunny weather. They can sit in their stuccos in the afternoon and cool off with a seltzer and a sandwich and watch the telly. You can't blame them. Arnie says, I guess it's okay for a couple of weeks, but sitting on your hands is not for me. Morey says, It's called retirement, Arnie. If you last that long, you get to retire. Arnie says, I'd rather keel over on the job.

POOLS

I'm waiting for Arnie. He pulls up to the curb. I get in. He says, How about a steak tonight? I say, You celebrating something? He says, Yeah, I'm talking to Blue Waters, a New York outfit, about a dealership. They're two young guys. They design and produce backyard swimming pools. They have a patented pool composition that dries in twenty-four hours and cuts labor costs by forty percent. It's a good possibility. I got to talk to Morey about backup. I say, What if you can't sell any? Arnie says, If it doesn't get off the ground, no one loses. Either you make money together or the deal is off. I say, Arnie, who's going to buy a pool in Buffalo with two or three months of summer? I don't think people in Buffalo swim a lot. Arnie says, Pools aren't for swimming. I say, What do you mean? Arnie says, A backyard pool is for floating, for sitting on a rubber tube holding a drink in one hand and waving at your neighbor with the other. I say, What's the neighbor got to do with it? Arnie says, People buy pools to impress those who don't have one. It's a status symbol. I say, What about kids? Arnie says, What about them?

THREE

Three brothers, including Arnie's father, agree to close the ladies' undergarment factory, sell the property and share the assets. They've been in business for thirty years and the old machinery is in need of constant repair. Arnie helps with the books and the retirement benefits for the few workers still there. They fired the accountant they thought was dipping into the profits, but in fact the business was becoming less profitable. They made plenty over the years and now they'll go their separate ways. Arnie says to me, they did okay for themselves. They didn't always write things down or consult each other. I think two bosses would have been better than three. Either none of them agreed or it was two against one. They yelled at each other long enough. They'll probably end up playing poker somewhere down in Florida. We laugh. Arnie says, I got enough out of it to buy a car.

A week later, Arnie pulls up to the house in a new Buick. He says, you want to go for a spin? I say, sure. He takes it out on the highway. Arnie says, what do you think? I say, Very nice. Why did you buy a Buick? Arnie says, The suspension. You float in this car. I could drive it all day. I say, Arnie, you're still young Why don't you drive half the time, and walk the other half? It would be good for you in the long run. Arnie says, There's no proof that driving a few hours a day is going to shorten your life. What actually shortens your life is too much exercise. It sounds weird, but it's a fact. I say, What makes it a fact? Arnie says, Okay, Buffalo's a snowy town in the winter, right? What causes most heart attacks in the winter? You guessed it, shoveling snow. You read about it every other day, somebody dying shoveling snow. That's one exercise you should stay away from. The position of the body against the weight of the shovel and the snow, and there you go. When's the last time you heard of someone having a heart attack driving a Buick?

FLYING

Arnie's real estate acqaintance Michael passed his flying tests. He has a license now. He calls Arnie and says, Hey fella, you going up with me, or you still chicken? Arnie says, Have you been up without a teacher? Michael says, Sure. Arnie says, I suppose it's possible. Michael says, I heard about your recent fishing trip to Canada in the C-46. Moe tells me you guys thought you were going down. Arnie says, It was a bumpy flight, let's put it that way. I prefer my Buick. Michael says, So what do you say? You still psyched out? Arnie says, You really have a license to fly? Michael says, Of course. Arnie says, I don't get it, Michael. What's the point of going around in circles? I wouldn't do it on the ground intentionally, so why do it up there? Michael says, I'll tell you why, Arnie. When you get past the suburbs into the countryside, you can fly low enough to survey the land parcels for sale that you'll never see driving around. Arnie says, Michael, I'm not a low-flying person. Take it all down, and if it comes to something, we'll work out a deal.

TREES

Morey says, Hey, Arnie, I see in the newspaper the Belle Village council wants to widen the main street. Arnie says, The shops won't go for it. They want the trees. Morey says, You're right, Arnie. It's the country flavor that attracts business there. Without trees, it will look like any other place. The nature club and the businesses will fight it. They got some big names in there. Arnie says, Morey, you like trees? Morey says, Sure, a tree, what's wrong with them? You get shade. Birds like them. Arnie says, They can damage property too. Morey says, Arnie, trees are on our side. Arnie says, What do you mean? Morey says, If they cut a tree down in front of a house, you can lose thousands. A tree is scenery. They add class. Look at the Martindale section and the money they pour into landscaping. They know the trees add to the property value, and I read recently that they help make fresh air, if you can believe it. Arnie says, When you walk your dog, you got to have a tree, right? Morey says, Yeah, that too.

AFTERNOON TEA

Arnie's cousin Dora and her husband are concerned about their neighbor, Mr. Dubin. She says to him, You should go to the afternoon tea at the center, Mr. Dubin. How long has it been since your wife passed away? You shouldn't sit alone. Mr. Dubin says, At my age, I need a woman like a hole in the wall. Dora says, It's Mondays and Wednesdays at two. You sit around with others who lost their partners and talk to someone. What have you got to lose? Mr. Dubin says, I talk to my dog. Dora says, So what does he say? Mr. Dubin says, Nothing, he listens. Dora says, They give you a cup of tea and a cookie, and there are big tables to sit at. You're not stuck with one person. Mr. Dubin says, Tea should be in a glass. Dora says, What's the difference? It tastes the same. If you want a glass, they'll give you a glass. Mr. Dubin says, Hymie the grocer goes. Dora says, So you can sit with Hymie. Mr. Dubin, do yourself a favor, it's free. Mr. Dubin says, If it's free, maybe I'll give it a try. Dora says, That's good. You meet Hymie and have tea and a cookie and look around, who knows?

On Monday, Mr. Dubin goes to the afternoon tea and sits at a big table with Hymie and five others. Hymie introduces Joe Dubin to the people at the table. Hymie says, Joe, where did you get the glass? Mr. Dubin says, I asked for a glass, so they gave me a glass. Mrs. Wald across the table says, I would like tea in a glass as well. I didn't know they had glasses. Two days later on Wednesday, there are both cups and glasses. Now Mr. Dubin comes every Monday and Wednesday and sits at the table with Mrs. Wald and talks. After a few visits to the center, he says to her, Mrs. Wald, you're a nice person to talk to, but you live too far from me. Mrs. Wald says, I drive. They both smile.

146

GORDON

Arnie is sitting at the diner counter having lunch. He says to the guy next to him, Excuse me, but I know you from somewhere. The guy next to him says, Yes, and I know you. I was one year ahead of you in high school. My name is Gordon Levy. Arnie says, Yeah, sure. Gordon Levy. So what are you up to, Gordon? Gordon says, Not much, and you? I hear you have a clothing store. Arnie says, Yeah, that was last year. I buy and sell real estate now. So what do you do, Gordon? Gordon says, I play the piano a few hours a day and I still live at home. Not a good combination. Fortunately, I'm going to a music conservatory in Philadelphia next semester. Arnie says, No kidding, Philadelphia. You're going to Philadelphia? Gordon says, I got a scholarship and it gets me out of here. I've been leaning on my folks too long. A lot of unspoken anxiety if you know what I mean. Arnie says, Well, you're not alone. Lots of guys live at home these days. Gordon says, Yeah, probably, but without pianos. Arnie says, So what did you play on a piano that gets you to Philly? Gordon says, I played a sonata for a jury and they liked it. Arnie says, A sonata, what's a sonata? Gordon says, A sonata is a composition written for the piano, in this case by a classical composer whose name is Franz Schubert. He lived a short life a more than a hundred years ago. You ever hear of him? Arnie says, No. So it's got to be longhair? Gordon says, Yeah, his compositions are considered extraordinary. Popular can be great, but you got to live by the rules if you want to be taken seriously. If I play exceptionally well, I might do concerts. Arnie says, So I guess you feel you got the goods. Gordon says, It's a long shot. It's hard work. I think I played this piece a few hundred times. Arnie says, It must have driven your folks nuts. You must really like this guy, what's his name? Gordon says, Let me put it this way, Arnie. If they like me, I make big money. Arnie says, Yeah, I follow you.

147

ANGELO

Angelo came from Sicily when he was a young man. His barbershop has been in the same location for years. There's two barber chairs. Angelo and his son, Vito, split the week, except for Friday and Saturday, when they're both there. Angelo is cutting Arnie's hair when his son Vito comes in with packages from the Italian grocery down the street. Angelo says, Hey, Vito, you got something for me? Vito says, Yeah, Pop, like every week. I'm your delivery boy. Arnie says, What, from the import grocery down the street? Vito says, Yeah, Arnie, he won't go there. It's old history. They insulted him or something, and he won't go there no more. When was that, Pop, how many years ago? I think the guy you said insulted you died five years ago, and the insult might have been five years before then. Angelo says, You're going there anyway. What, you want company? Vito says to Arnie, The people in the store come from Potenza, in the Boot. They're not Sicilian. Vito and Arnie laugh. Angelo says, You know Arnie, I swear, it's the only place in the city you see flies in the window in winter. Arnie says, They do a hell of a business. Angelo says, Dumb luck.

A few days later, Vito's working in the barbershop and his father Angelo phones. Vito says, What's up, Pop? Angelo says, Vito, there's a car blocking the driveway. It's been there over an hour. Vito says, Have it towed, Pop. Don't lose time over that. Angelo says, Yeah, right, and hangs up. Ten minutes later Angelo calls back. Angelo says, Vito, I can't find "cops" in the yellow pages. Vito laughs and says, Pop, what's the matter with you? It's "police," not "cops." Look up "police." Vito laughs and says, You're something else.

THE PLAN

I'm in New York. Arnie calls from Buffalo. He says, Do you want to go to Utah? I say, What's up? He says, The Defense Department needs uranium. I'm coming to New York to look at Geiger counters and other equipment. Are you interested? I say, Yeah, I'm interested, but . . . He says, Never mind the buts, I'll explain it to you when I get there. Arnie arrives. He looks like an executive. He says, You got a suit coat? We go down to someplace in midtown, up to the tenth floor. Two guys are standing around looking like Arnie, businesslike, smiles, good morning sir, and all that. Arnie says, I would like to see your latest Geiger counter equipment. They talk, exchange information, and then we leave. We go downtown and pick up a big tent and some camping equipment. On the way he tells me about the jeep he's going to pick up and how we'll prospect on federal land in Utah. I tell Arnie that I heard uranium was radioactive, and that the stuff can kill you. He says, We'll have special handling devices. I say, You mean gloves? He says, They're not just ordinary gloves. I tell Arnie I like the idea about the open spaces, but the rest seems too complicated. Arnie says, If you think life is difficult, that's what it's going to be. There are simple ways of doing complicated things. He explains the plan. We'll drive a jeep across a vast area. I'll do the driving, he says. Meanwhile you'll have the Geiger counter on your lap. We'll tie your door open so you can extend the counter over the ground. It's like a grass trimmer. When the counter lights up and begins to tick, we'll stop, carefully lift the uranium from its cavity, place it in a bucket in the back, and take off. Probably what we can lift, buddy, will make us rich for the rest of our lives.

Arnie leaves town. He'll get back to me. His girlfriend tells him that if he goes west, she's through with him. He must have told her the plan. He calls and says, Let's put the plan on hold for a while. It's a winner, he says. Just give me a little time and I'll get back to you. A couple months later, Arnie is managing a ladies' apparel shop. He calls me and says he'll be in New York the next day, would I like to have dinner with him and Jascha Heifetz? I say, What are you talking about? He says, I got a meeting in the afternoon. I'll pick you up at seven. We go to a fancy restaurant near Times Square. He introduces me to Jascha Heifetz. I didn't know there were two of them. This one is in ladies' apparel. The dinner is great.

MANSION

Moe drives into a rest stop for a bit of shut-eye. He dreams he's driving a moving van with two helpers in the front seat. They pull into the driveway of a big mansion. They go inside and begin hauling out the furniture and putting it in the van. Moe says, Take everything. One helper says, You want the mirrors and drapes, too? Moe says, Yeah, the mirror and drapes, too. The other helper says, You want the kitchen appliances? Moe says, Yeah, take the kitchen appliances. They fill the van and drive off. They pull up in front of an empty store. They haul everything into the store. Moe says, Now I have a store. I'll call it Mansion Furniture. Moe wakes up and eats the the other half of his pastrami sandwich and drives off.

LODGE

It's mid-September. Arnie's invited to an Adirondack lodge for
the weekend, by an executive with Elastics Company in New
York. He drives to the lodge. At the end of the road is a big
1920s hotel for the well-to-do, updated to suit present needs.
He checks in and returns to the main hall with its soft leather
chairs and central fireplace, aglow with a log fire. Two men
in gray coats are taking orders for drinks and food. It's mid-
afternoon. He'll sit around and be sociable tonight. He walks
down to a pier on the lake. Small motorboats are available
for guests, equipped with oars, life jacket, rain gear, rod and
reel, an assortment of lures, and a chest containing food and
drink. He talks to the attendant about the fishing, hops in the
boat, pulls the cord, and glides the craft into the vast calm
waters. He looks at the rounded mountain and the colors of
the valley, as if he's been here before, and recalls a day at the
art museum with Sultz, seeing a Thomas Cole painting of
the same region. He takes the boat across the lake, cuts the
engine, and casts his line close to the shore. Almost imme-
diately, his rod bends slightly, and he reels in a half-pound
brook trout. He carefully detaches the barb, lowers the fish
into the water, and watches it swim off. He's aware that his
thoughts are taking him somewhere he's never been before.

INDEX OF STORIES

154

LIST OF ILLUSTRATIONS

All illustrations are by Philip Sultz. Except as noted, they are mixed-media collages.

ACKNOWLEDGMENTS

Thank you to Peter Rooney, who introduced my stories to David Fabricant of Laboratory Books, and to David for his masterful editing and wonderful enthusiasm. These stories would still be looking for a home without you. Thanks also to Stephen Dixon, who has encouraged me over the years to keep writing, and has been a champion of my work.

Thanks to the circle of family and friends who provided inspiration for these characters and stories. The vividness of my memories of those early years has fueled the journey of this book.

And thanks to my daughter Heather, who is my first editor and manager, and represents me with great clarity and thoughtfulness; and to my daughter Jennifer and my wife Jan, whose invaluable suggestions made the book better, and whose support makes everything possible.

ABOUT THE AUTHOR

Philip Sultz is an artist and writer whose visual work was represented for over three decades by Allan Stone Gallery in New York. He was a recipient of a National Endowment for the Arts Fellowship, and has exhibited extensively. Sultz's poetry and prose have been published in numerous journals, including *Fifth Wednesday* and *The Hopkins Review*. An extensive collection of his photographs of western settlement life is held at the Jackson Hole Historical Society, and he was an early contributor of articles and photographs to *The American West*, the journal of the Western History Association. Sultz taught in higher education for thirty years at Kansas City Art Institute, Rhode Island School of Design, and Webster University, where he is professor emeritus. Born in Buffalo, New York, he lives in Maine.